R. Le
B 1947
75¢

Also by Robert Nathan

NOVELS

One More Spring
Jonah
Road of Ages
The Enchanted Voyage
Winter in April
Journey of Tapiola
Portrait of Jennie
They Went On Together
Tapiola's Brave Regiment
The Sea-Gull Cry
But Gently Day

AN OMNIBUS

The Barly Fields — containing these novels:
The Fiddler in Barly
The Woodcutter's House
The Bishop's Wife
The Orchid
There Is Another Heaven

POEMS

Selected Poems
A Winter Tide
Dunkirk (included in *The Darkening Meadows*)
Morning in Iowa
The Darkening Meadows

NON–FICTION

Journal for Josephine

THESE are Borzoi Books, published in
New York by Alfred A. Knopf

Mr. Whittle and the Morning Star

Mr. Whittle

AND THE

Morning Star

ROBERT NATHAN

But that which ye have already, hold fast till I
come. . . . And I will give him the morning star.
REVELATION ii, 25, 28

Alfred · A · Knopf : NEW YORK · 1947

For Janet

Mr. Whittle and the Morning Star

CHAPTER

One

It was on the second of May, in the morning,
that Robert Whittle, Professor of History at
Caraway College, decided that the world was
coming to an end. Spring was in its earliest leaf;
on Elm Street the trees were just beginning to
burst their buds, and the forsythia blossomed on
the lawns. The sweet air of morning, the gentle
light, a little misty, yellow as a buttercup in the
sun, blue as a cornflower in the shade, washed the
quiet streets of Rivertown and the campus of
Caraway College, where young men and women,
carrying their books in layers like so many slabs
of brick, walked in a morning dream from class
to class.

It was not only coming, thought Mr. Whittle,
but it was coming very soon, it was almost here.

He sat at the breakfast table, and looked at

his wife Amanda, and at his twelve-year-old daughter Lucinda, who was home from school because of there being chicken-pox in the seventh grade. At the thought that the three of them would not be together very much longer, he experienced a moment of panic and a feeling of intense regret. However, there was no use fooling himself.

"Good-by," he said.

His wife looked up in surprise. "Do you have to go so early?" she asked.

Mr. Whittle did not reply directly. The foremost physicists in the country, plus the heads of the army and navy, all agreed that the end of the world was coming and that it was merely a matter of time. They did not all agree on the time, however, many of them believing that it would not take place until after they were dead; to these, Mr. Whittle replied that they were whistling in the dark. Only the English did not believe that anything could happen to the British Empire.

Looking up from the headlines of the newspaper, which was filled with bad news, Mr. Whittle remarked in a grave and affectionate tone:

"We are doomed, like the dinosaurs and the Neanderthal men, of whom the last example was probably the hero Gilgamesh, in the Sumerian legend of four thousand B.C."

"Why are we doomed?" asked Lucinda, leaning forward to see what was happening to Dick Tracy, the detective in the comic strip, on the under side of the newspaper in her father's hands.

"Because we have learned the wrong things," said Mr. Whittle. "We have learned to explode the atom, which is to say the stuff that we are made of; but we have not learned to get along with each other. So we shall all explode together."

"Robert," said his wife, "I wish you would be serious, and tell me whether to have lamb chops or pork for supper."

"Is there any apple sauce left over?" asked the professor.

"No," said Mrs. Whittle.

"Lamb, then," said Mr. Whittle. A moment later he added:

"I was never more serious in my life."

"Are we going to drown, like Noah and the Flood?" asked his daughter, her eyes glued to the back side of the paper.

"Not this time," said Mr. Whittle. "This time we are going to blow up like a firecracker."

"I think that would be super," said Lucinda, who was not paying very much attention to what her father was saying.

And she added, with satisfaction:

"Dick Tracy is in trouble again."

Mrs. Whittle sighed. "I must buy the child some dresses for the summer," she said. "She has grown again, nothing will fit her."

"Oh, crow!" groaned Lucinda.

"Can't she be blown up in an old dress?" asked Mr. Whittle a little irritably.

"I suppose she could," replied his wife, "but if we're all to explode together, there's no use trying to save, is there?"

Mrs. Whittle was a practical soul whose motto was to do the best she could with what she had. This included Mr. Whittle, her daughter, her seven-room house with mortgage, the 1937 Chevrolet coupé, and Mr. Whittle's small salary. It is true that at the end of twenty years Mr. Whittle could expect to retire on a pension, but Mrs. Whittle did not expect to live that long. Not that she looked for the world to end; the world, she thought, would last longer than she would. But sometimes, lying alone in the dark at night while Mr. Whittle snored in a small way at her side, she imagined that she was suffering from an incurable disease, like cancer, or some unknown trouble. Death, she thought; there it is, I can't escape it. The minute I was born, I couldn't escape it, no matter what I did. I am simply a mouse in a trap. Then she felt sorry for herself, and for Lucinda and Mr. Whittle, and had to sing, to keep her spirits up. She sang under her breath, in a whisper, so as not to wake up Mr. Whittle: "Alas, that spring should vanish with the rose." When she got to the high note, she just imagined it.

In the morning she felt fine again, and ready to take care of everything.

Or sometimes in the long, spring evenings, with the damp sweet smell of earth around her, and the robins busy in the grass, she thought of the many, many lovers long ago, who had watched the spring, had seen the leaves unfurl and the lilac bloom, and who had grown old and died . . . and still the birds sang and the roses blossomed. It made her sad, and comforted her at the same time. But when she tried to mention something of the kind to Mr. Whittle, he knew all about it.

"The sense of a continuing existence was very strong among most of the ancient peoples," he said, "particularly the Chinese. The Greeks, on the other hand, were egocentrics, and did not go in for ancestor worship, like the Romans."

This explanation struck Mrs. Whittle as a little dry, considering the feelings she had tried to express.

As for Lucinda, death was completely meaningless and only happened to other people. However, when she realized that the whole world might blow up, she felt a twinge of alarm, and exclaimed:

"Jeepers."

For it occurred to her that in that case she would miss the long summer vacation.

She lived for immediate things, for small pleasures greedily devoured and soon forgotten, for the sudden moment of joy . . . for the long hours of waiting. At the thought of being fitted to a new dress, she experienced an almost physical nausea.

"It's so boring," she exclaimed. "You just stand around, and stand around."

"And what else," asked Mrs. Whittle, "have you got to do that's so important?"

She had nothing to do, and everything. There were her friends Marian and Ellen down the street; they could play games together, or read the comics, or simply walk up and down and feel the importance, the rapture, of growing up. And there was the new boy, Ralph Wender, who lived on the corner, and was fourteen, and smooth. This was only to say that he was new, and therefore still to be explored, and put in his proper place; actually, he was awkward and lumpy as a calf. And finally there was the spring itself, fresh, mild, sweet, and full of dreams, like a bowl full of cookies. Merely to dream was to do something — something important, she couldn't say what. . . .

Mrs. Whittle knew her daughter, and sympathized with her; she saw herself at twelve, and remembered what life had looked like. But she was thirty-two now, with the housework to do, and she was tired of letting down hems; besides, there were no hems left any more, to let down. "A plain cotton print, I think," she said; "something washable."

"Couldn't I have a dirndl," asked Lucinda, "like Ellen?"

"Certainly not," said Mrs. Whittle. "Ellen's father is vice president of a bank."

Mr. Whittle gazed thoughtfully at his family, across the breakfast dishes. It was true, he had not given them very much — though he had tried hard. He wondered for a moment if he had tried hard enough; but what more could he have done? He had hoped for something better than Caraway College, but it had been a vain hope. And he did make a living, and have a sort of dignity

— not as much as Ellen's father, of course, who was a vice president of the Farmer's Loan and Trust, and drove to work every morning in his own Cadillac. Still, it was all right to be a professor; and somebody had to do the teaching after all. Well, it was almost over now — almost finished and done with: soon there would be no college, and no bank, and no vice president of anything. He thought of Dr. Amadeus Thirkel, President of Caraway College; it would be a great shock to Dr. Thirkel not to be President any more — to be nothing but a wisp of vapor, somewhere in the void.

His mind strayed into dreamy speculation. How hard it was to imagine nothingness — to realize, for instance, that no one would ever remember anything that had happened. To think that music and the alphabet and noodle soup would simply disappear into thin air, never to be mentioned anywhere again — and after such a short existence, geologically speaking. All man's knowledge, from the wheel to penicillin. . . . And love, the whisper and the dream, the kiss, the sigh, the touch of hands, the play of limbs and cunning joints; eyes to see with, noses for smells, tongues for taste, the miraculous organization of nerves . . . all, all to vanish like time into the infinite. . . .

Who would ever remember the spring, with its lilacs and its dandelions? Or the speeches of Cicero, or Winston Churchill?

No more than anyone remembered the love song of the dodo. If there ever was a dodo.

"I'm sorry about the apple sauce," said Mrs. Whittle. "If you like, I'll try to get some more, though nobody seems to have any in town."

"Nobody will know there ever was such a thing as apple sauce," said Mr. Whittle soberly.

Mrs. Whittle looked at him sharply; there were moments when she found her husband quite irritating. "Are you going to keep this up all day?" she demanded. "I asked you a simple question about apple sauce."

"I'm sorry," said Mr. Whittle humbly; "I was thinking about something else. By all means, get some if you can."

Mrs. Whittle turned to her daughter. "Run along upstairs, Lucinda," she said briskly, "and make your bed. I want to talk to your father." Then she began to gather the breakfast dishes together. But before she left the room, she remarked:

"Do you think it wise to put such ideas into the child's head?"

Mr. Whittle gazed at her in surprise. "What ideas?" he asked.

"All this nonsense about the end of the world," said Mrs. Whittle.

"I assure you," said Mr. Whittle, "it isn't nonsense at all."

"Very well," said Mrs. Whittle. "But is it necessary to give the child hysterics?"

"Hysterics?" cried Mr. Whittle in astonishment. "She never even listened to me."

"Perhaps not," said his wife, "but she'll have nightmares just the same. She's at a very emotional age."

With her arms full of dishes, she started for the kitchen, but turned at the door, to give her husband an enigmatic look. "So you really think the end of the world is at hand?" she asked.

Mr. Whittle nodded gravely. It was amazing,

he thought, how young Amanda looked, almost as young as when he had married her. She was a little stouter, perhaps, but he was used to it; and besides, her girdle helped to hold her together. He noticed that she still had her dimples when she smiled. "It is simply a matter of time," he said. "The means are there."

"In that case," said Amanda, "I think we should all do exactly as we please, and enjoy ourselves to the hilt."

With this strange remark, she went into the kitchen, and closed the door, leaving her husband staring out of the window at the bright spring morning.

CHAPTER

Two

THE CLASS in History IV (A General Outline of History from the Fall of Rome to the French Revolution) drowsed through the long, spring hour. Outside, the voices of a few students sounded across the fresh-cut grass, and footsteps crunched on the gravel. Time, like a tide of air, moved slowly over the earth, and the faded blue sky poured down its quiet light on Rivertown.

Mr. Whittle, from the raised platform on which he sat behind his desk, looked down at the class. He saw rows of heads bent over their notes, poised and anxious pencils, crossed ankles in cotton or wool; he saw the multicolored shirts of the young men, open at the neck and out at the bottom, and the quieter sweaters and skirts of the young women. He saw dark hair and light, hair-ribbons, scuffed shoes, inky fingers, and notebooks; and now and then a face, lifted blankly, or with hope, in his direction. He saw eyes and noses, but he could not see into the hearts or minds of any of his students.

Still, he thought, why should that depress me? Do they see into my mind? No indeed; and it is a good thing, too, for if they did, they would be very much alarmed.

"In France," he said, "the works of Voltaire and of Rousseau had already aroused a lively interest in the new ideas." The pencils moved, the line of notes flowed on.

What had he thought about at that age? — at eighteen, at nineteen? Life . . . the leap of spirit, like a salmon bent upstream, the wish blown into the wind like dandelion seed . . . the shaken heart, the running joy. . . . And what was he thinking about now?

Death.

How could that have happened in so few years?

How indeed? One day the world was full of light and hope; and the next, both hope and light were gone. Suddenly and quietly, at vast expense, and to save their own lives, men had learned to turn their enemies into radio-active clouds, into poisonous gases and destructive whirlwinds. It was a desperate paradox, for in learning to destroy others they had invited destruction upon themselves.

Only the firm heart should have such knowledge, only the complete and satisfied spirit. But men's spirits had remained as before, as full of gravel as a chicken's gizzard.

His glance traveled to the bright, golden head of Penelope Andrews, seated in the front row; it took in the gracefully bent young neck, the swelling breasts under the taut green sweater, the rounded knees under the short plaid skirt. You, Penelope Andrews, he said, what is there in your heart but hunger and confusion? Do you think of anything but today and tomorrow? Or of anyone but yourself — and perhaps some teen-aged youth with his shirt tails hanging out? . . .

Penelope Andrews did not look up. Her pencil raced across the paper, to get everything down. She had just heard Professor Whittle remark:

"The French and Indian wars in the forests of North America were only a microcosm of the greater struggle raging across the continent of Europe."

Her little tongue peeped out for a moment between her lips, warm and red as strawberries in the sun. She would have to ask somebody what microcosm meant.

Mr. Whittle thought of his wife Amanda, who had been young, too, when he had met her. He remembered the delicious torment of the first year, the mystery of the young woman concealed among her dresses and her dreams. He remembered the rapture and the pain of their courtship. . . . What was it Amanda had said? — Let us do exactly as we please, and enjoy ourselves to the hilt. . . .

And what would please *you* most, Penelope Andrews? The shadowy evening, sweet with grass and the last songs of birds? Or the windy hill in the sun, or the lapping of lake water? Or the butterfly-cloud of youth, drifting in the

light . . . to rise and fall in the warm currents
of air, to know nothing, to think of nothing, only
to feel, to hunger, to embrace . . . ?

An abyss wider than night and all its stars
seemed to extend between them, to separate them
from each other. We do not even have an interest in history together, he thought; and as for
what I might have taught you, you will not live
long enough to appreciate it.

Penelope Andrews drew the tip of her tongue
back into her mouth again. There was nothing so
dull as history — the story of things that had
happened long ago. Who cared what had happened long ago — to other people? It was
only today that mattered, that was vital and important — today, when the latest songs kept
running through her head, the newest dance
steps lifting and swaying in her knees, and all
her mind and heart taken up with Marian
Greene's dark-haired brother Marvin Greene —
Marvin the careless, the dashing, the divine. . . .

If only History were over, and she could walk
to Math with Marvin, the long way round, out
past the gym and Dakin Hall. . . .

She looked up momentarily, her eyes soft with dreams, to find Professor Whittle staring at her. It confused her; blushing, she looked down at her lap; was her skirt too high above her knees? But a moment later, she glanced up at him again, from under her long, dusky lashes.

He was looking at her still, and with such a strange expression . . . unfathomable, she told herself. He was an odd little man, she thought, smaller than Marvin, and of course endlessly older. Old enough to be her father, she supposed. What did he want? He had rather a wistful look; he must be a pathetic creature.

Raising her head, she stared him full in the face, with sudden, wide, golden eyes.

Mr. Whittle was talking about the meeting of the States-General in Paris in 1789. But really he was saying farewell to mankind; behind the façade of the French Revolution, he was apostrophizing his generation.

You had everything, he cried out silently; all that was needed was for your hearts to keep up with your heads. Think how far you went in science and discovery; you were masters of earth

20

and air. Even the pox had given in to you; you had conquered disease, hunger, heat and cold, distance, silence, and the desert. There remained only fear, hate, and death; and these have finally done you in. Was it worth dying, to remain an Englishman? or to keep others from becoming Russians, or democrats?

You were gods; from the point of view of an ant, or a spaniel, your powers were so tremendous as to appear divine. Truly, you harnessed the lightning, you made use of elements, you discovered the firmament, and invented music. There was nothing you could not do, nothing that was too much for you, except to get along with yourselves and with each other. That was the one thing that was out of the question.

You were cruel; and in the end it was your cruelty that destroyed you. Always rude, mischievous, and overbearing, you became hysterical, and no longer cared whom you struck. Man himself became your enemy, for a number of reasons . . . because of the length of his nose or the color of his hair, because he had more money than you, or because he had less . . . for the slightest of reasons, or for no reason at all. That was the end of you; for you forgot that you, too, were man.

If you had not known all this, there still might have been some help for you; shaken by surprise, shocked by your own situation, you still might have reformed your ways. But unfortunately, it was all known, it was an old story in the newspapers. You were like the dinosaurs who watched their relatives sink into the tar pits two million years ago, with horrid cries and bellowings — and who allowed themselves to be swallowed up, a few days later. They brought down with them only the lesser beasts and insects of the period; you, on the contrary, will bring down the solar system.

"This young lieutenant of artillery," said Mr. Whittle out loud, "was a Corsican; his name, Napoleon Bonaparte."

It was at this moment that his eyes, which had not really been looking at anything in particular, encountered the full, deep gaze of Penelope Andrews. At first Mr. Whittle had no feeling about it at all; then his heart gave a sudden

jump, followed by a lurch. It seemed to him almost as though he had received an electric shock
of some sort.

For a moment or two, Mr. Whittle remained
spellbound and motionless. Then he looked away,
narrowed his eyes, cleared his throat, and began
to breathe again; however, he could not put that
direct look, which seemed almost to reach out
and touch him, out of his mind. He did not know
whether to look at Miss Andrews again, or not;
he would have liked to do so, but he was re-
strained by a feeling of delicacy and a sense of
his position; he felt that it might appear better
not to have noticed anything.

A bell rang somewhere in the building, re-
cording the end of the hour, and Mr. Whittle
closed the book on his desk.

"The end of the world is at hand," he said.
"Class is dismissed."

Cheerfully, with a clatter of chairs and shoes,
the class rose and trooped out, without stopping
to inquire what Mr. Whittle had meant by his
remark.

"The history of the world," said Miss Woy-

23

czinsky to her companion as they went out of the door, "is the history of the Catholic Church." Her companion, a young gentleman named O'Leary, whose father was a mill worker, replied simply:

"The history of the world will be written in Russian."

Penelope Andrews hurried down the wide brownstone steps of the lecture hall, without stopping to gossip with anyone. And presently she and Marvin Greene were strolling down the pathway near the gymnasium, between the forsythia bushes. Marvin looked very handsome in his woolen shirt with its green, red, and purple squares, open at the neck, and hanging out of his britches. His dark hair, plastered down with water, and with a preparation of oil and cologne, seemed to shine in the sun; and his face expressed repose and satisfaction. They walked with their fingers interlaced, swinging their clasped hands between them.

But presently something in the way he held her hand sent a sudden chill through her.

"What's the matter, Marve?" she asked softly.

24

"Nothing."

As a matter of fact, nothing was the matter; and at the same time, everything: he was simply beginning to grow tired of her. It was not her fault, and he didn't quite know it yet himself; but the truth was, he wanted something more exciting, and possibly less beautiful. Spring was a time for new things, for hunting, and for danger; the only danger with Penelope was that he might have to marry her some day if he kept on. Penelope was a tame rabbit.

She disengaged her fingers quietly. How silly the forsythia looked, the sad little buttery blossoms. . . . The morning stretched out ahead, flat and endless, full of dismal hours. . . .

"Well," he said, "what did old Whittle talk about today?"

"I forget," she said.

Old Whittle. . . . He had colored, ever so faintly, when she had looked at him. He must be almost thirty-five — or even forty; was it possible to have feelings at that age? That is to say — thoughts about women? She tossed her head; she was indignant, and faintly shocked. "He said

25

something about the end of the world," she said. "I don't know what he meant."

"He was just trying to be smart," said Marvin. "All the profs like to say something they think is smart."

"That's right," said Penelope. "Half the time you can't ever figure them at all."

She was silent for a moment, in spiritual communion with Marvin, who was her ideal. At last she asked timidly:

"Are you going to take me to the movie tonight?"

He looked away, uncomfortably. "Well, now, I don't know," he said. "I've got a date with some fellows."

She nodded; for she had half expected something like that. She was unhappy, and in some illusive way she blamed Mr. Whittle for it. He had no business looking at her like that, she thought.

Men were all horrid.

At the same time, it comforted her to think that Mr. Whittle was also, perhaps, unhappy. And she looked forward to Monday, to the next class in History IV, when she would have a chance to see him again. This time, she thought, she would give him a really deep look; it was amusing to see him blush and turn away. It was rather exciting to know that she was able to do things like that — even to old men like Mr. Whittle.

Still, if Marvin no longer cared for her, her heart would be broken.

Three

AMANDA was cleaning house. Surrounded by pails, brooms, mops, and dustpans, her hair covered with a bandanna, and an old apron tied around her waist, she scrubbed, polished, and dusted the small cottage, including the room which Mr. Whittle liked to think of as his study. This room, in which he kept his books and his papers, his framed diploma from Iowa State, his pipes, and a plated silver bowl presented to him by the students of the Gropper School for Boys, when he had left that institution to assume his duties at Caraway, gave him a sense if not of security, at least of continuity; but its floors were washed every week, along with the rest of the house. For Amanda did everything as thoroughly as she could. She worked hard, not only from necessity, but in defiance of her parents, who had never approved of her marriage and still expected it to come to a bad end after fourteen years.

It had not come to a bad end; but as the years went round faster and faster, it seemed to be held together by some sort of centrifugal force, rather than by joy or some other emotion. It seemed to Amanda that she remembered joy; it was like the summers she remembered from her youth, fragrant, serene, and far away. The summers went on, they had not ended; but she had to admit that they had changed, like her hair, which she noticed had grown darker. Nothing ever ended, she thought; things only seemed to end, like daylight or dark; next morning, or next evening, there it was again. Over and over, over and over.

So it was unlikely that the world was coming to an end, even if Robert thought so. Since he did nothing about the house anyway, it made no difference one way or another what he thought; the cleaning and cooking would have to go on as usual. She smiled a little wearily as she imagined what Robert would say if there were no dinner ready for him when he came home; he would certainly object very much to being starved; she was sure he would resent having to be blown up on an empty stomach.

Still, she had to admit, the world had changed since she was a child. And on her knees, in front of a little pool of soapy water, she tried to think what it was that had gone wrong.

For one thing, it seemed to her that the world she remembered had been a world of good feeling and freedom. But when she stopped to think about it, she wondered if she had not simply been too young to know what was going on. That's it, she thought; the children never know what is happening; even in a war, they are only concerned with their own affairs. That is why it is so hard to be a parent. I'm sure that Lucinda believes this is the best possible time to be alive — which after all is a fortunate thing, when you come to think of it.

Amanda had a busy day ahead of her; there was always more to do than there was time for. After the housework was done, she went to market, and stood in line to buy three chops, a loaf of spongy bread, four tomatoes in celophane, a dozen eggs, and a box of matches. There was no butter, margarine, mayonnaise, olive oil, sugar, flour, or shortening in market; no fish, soap flakes, lettuce, or fresh vegetables. Then she went home, to cook lunch; in the afternoon she took Lucinda downtown to buy a dress, and then there was dinner to get; and after dinner she went over her accounts for the day, mended clothes and darned socks, and wrote a letter to her parents, full of friendly information.

Meanwhile, in his study, Mr. Whittle read the evening paper, and the latest reports from Europe and South America; and Lucinda listened to the radio, on which the noblest themes of the great composers were presented as banal love songs.

On Sundays Mrs. Whittle went to church, not because she believed in God — or disbelieved in Him either, for that matter — but for the sense of goodness and for the quiet, and because it was a change from the rest of the week. She no longer tried to take Mr. Whittle or Lucinda with her; Mr. Whittle had gone for a while at first because it was expected of him as a professor at the college, but then he had given it up because, as he said, you could believe in history, or in Divine Providence, but not in both; and as for Lucinda, Mrs. Whittle had realized that God was something completely beyond her daughter's imagination. She had tried telling her the story of Jesus, but it had only seemed to confuse her; Lucinda could not understand how Jesus could be God's Son, and be poor, and not have everything He wanted. As Mr. Whittle pointed out, that was something that had puzzled the Jews, too, in those days.

Mrs. Whittle was further handicapped by not wanting her daughter to be afraid of God, because she didn't believe in bringing up a child in fear of its Creator. And Lucinda could see no reason to love Him just because He had created her; why, she might as well be expected to love her father for feeding her and sending her to school. As a matter of fact, Lucinda did not love anything or anybody; but she was attracted to Van Johnson, and Peter Lawford.

She also hoped to make an impression on

Ralph Wender, who lived at the corner, but that was on a more direct and personal plane.

Now, on this particular Sunday evening, she sat on the floor in one corner of the Whittle dining room with her friend Ellen Blaney, reading the comics, and trying to decide who was more divine, Mr. Stettinius, or Dick Tracy, the detective.

Supper was over, and the dishes were cleared away; in the living room, Ellen's father and mother were visiting with the Whittles. Seated on opposite sides of the small fireplace, Mr. Blaney and Mr. Whittle discussed local politics and the state of the country, which Mr. Blaney believed to be sound, but in the wrong hands. Side by side on the sofa, Mrs. Blaney and Amanda sewed, and talked about the price of food and the scarcity of linen, nylon, soap, and rickrack for curtains. They were old friends and they were not afraid that by complaining about things they would lose each other's respect. At the same time, Amanda could not forget that Alfred Blaney was vice president of a bank, and could afford to pay high prices for everything;

under the circumstances, it almost seemed as though Ruth Blaney ought not to complain so much.

"The trouble," said Mr. Blaney, leaning back and looking thoughtfully at his cigar, "lies in the fact that we have put too high a value on ordinary services. Naturally, during the war, we couldn't help ourselves; we had to get the work done, no matter what it cost. But now comes the problem: who is going to pay for it? No one wants less, and everybody wants more. . . ."

Naturally, thought Mr. Whittle: no one has ever wanted less, except the Early Christians, or the hermits of the Thebaid. And if they wanted less, it was only because they expected to get more later, in heaven.

"The government," said Mr. Blaney, "has got itself into a mess. Fourteen years of the Democrats — fourteen years of giving in to labor. . . . Now we've got the bill for it. The question is: what's going to happen to money? Inflation. . . ."

"Money," said Mr. Whittle, "will always be worth less, because more people will have it. The fortune of Crœsus, which consisted of the greater part of the world's wealth at that time, was comparatively small, by modern standards. A century ago, to have a million dollars was to be a millionaire. On the other hand, servants received only eight dollars a month. Today it is barely possible to keep alive with a million dollars."

"I wouldn't say that," remarked Mr. Blaney.

Mr. Whittle, who received thirty-two hundred dollars a year from the college, continued: "What has happened is that we have discovered what it is like not to be millionaires. Already that is a sobering experience. Now we are going to learn that we cannot get along without somebody to do our work for us."

"We all of us have our work to do," said Mr. Blaney; and he added generously: "you too."

"The man who collects my garbage is more important to me than the president of a bank," said Mr. Whittle.

"I wouldn't say that," said Mr. Blaney. "That's getting things a little mixed up."

"Things *are* mixed up," said Mr. Whittle calmly. He added: "I suppose you think that people should be paid according to how rare they are. But it is precisely these rare people that we can get along without, at the lowest level. On the other hand, without the common people we could not get along at all, on any level."

"That is communism, I believe," said Mr. Blaney sternly.

"So it is," said Mr. Whittle, "and since I am not a communist, and do not want to live on the lowest level, I ought to do all I can to keep these common people from knowing how important they are to me. But that is a difficult position for me to be in, for it obliges me to refuse to admit the truth to another human being. It is just as difficult for the communists, who do not want to live on the lowest level either."

"We shall have to live on the lowest level soon," said Mrs. Blaney, stitching away, "because everything has gone so high."

"In any case," said Mr. Whittle, "it will not last much longer."

Amanda looked around the pleasant little parlor which she had spent so many hours cleaning. From the dining room came the sound of whispers and aimless laughter, as the two little girls compared their experiences and their opinions. Mrs. Blaney took little stitches in her sewing; Mr. Blaney puffed comfortably on his cigar; and the clock ticked quietly away on the mantelpiece.

"Robert thinks that the world is coming to an end," she said, smiling.

Mrs. Blaney delicately bit her thread off at the bottom, and made a new knot. "Does he really?" she remarked. And turning to her husband, she asked:

"Have you heard anything about that, Alfred?"

"No," said Mr. Blaney. "But it will come to an end all right, if Congress don't stop passing laws against business, like they've been doing for the past fourteen years."

The lamplight fell across Amanda's face, making a shadow under her eyes, lighting up the firm chin, the quick and delicate fingers as they pushed the needle into the cloth and drew it out again. That's a pretty woman, thought Mr. Blaney; but she works too hard.

It was not the first time that he had noticed

Amanda's good looks. He had known her a long time, ever since Mr. Whittle had come to Caraway, and Amanda had put her daughter in the Rivertown School, in the same grade as Ellen. It must have been a matter of five or six years. Five, anyway.

We all work too hard, he thought with satisfaction. But then, for some reason, it occured to him that he was getting older, and that he had never done anything very exciting in his life. He had gone through school and high school, and into the banking business; he had been successful, but there was no heat to it, nothing to think about in a secret way when he was alone. In the fifteen years he had been married to Ruth, he had never kissed another woman. And of course Ruth had never kissed anybody else, either. Still, she was not what you'd call a pretty woman; in fact, when you came right down to it, she was a little musty. He wondered if perhaps he was a little musty, too; but he didn't feel musty.

He wondered if Amanda was still in love with her husband. It shouldn't have made him feel

unhappy, but it did. He didn't want the Whittles
to be in love with each other.

For a moment he thought: Suppose the world
were going to end tomorrow, or next week . . .
what would I be doing, at my desk, at the bank?

He began to perspire a little, and wiped his
forehead with his handkerchief. What was the
matter with him? He didn't want to die, he
thought, without ever having done anything . . . without ever having done anything
to any other woman except his wife.

Outside in the May night, the moths fluttered
softly against the windows, and the June bugs
pitted against the glass like little stones. Mrs.
Blaney sewed placidly on; and in the dining
room, Lucinda said to Ellen:

"What do you think, Hilda Cornwaller wears
reinforced drawers, and she's almost thirteen
years old.

"Isn't that dumb?"

"Oh please," exclaimed Ellen; "really!" And
the two little girls burst into vacuous laughter.

CHAPTER

Four

On Monday, Mr. Whittle was called into the President's office, for a consultation. He found Dr. Thirkel seated behind his desk, on which stood a penholder in the form of a football player, and a framed motto done in needle-point, which read: The Reward Of Learning Is Wisdom. Mr. Whittle sat down, but he did not cross his legs, because he was nervous. "Yes?" he asked.

Dr. Thirkel at once tried to put him at his ease. "Well, Whittle," he remarked in a genial way, "how are things going?"

"Very well, I believe," said Mr. Whittle uncertainly.

He had often thought that as a grown-up man and a professor of history he ought not to be afraid of anything, and that when Dr. Thirkel spoke to him he would remain calm and in command of the situation. But the truth was, he was unable to face authority in any form without blinking. The most dismal thoughts raced through his mind, he saw himself a failure, disgraced, without money or position, and he already felt sorry for his family.

There was no reason for this, which made it all the more difficult to control.

Dr. Thirkel leaned forward across his desk and, clasping his hands together, exclaimed:

"I do not mind telling you that I am very much .pleased with what you are doing in the history department."

At once Mr. Whittle began to breathe again, grew pale, smiled, and cautiously crossed his knees. "Thank you," he murmured.

"Whittle," said Dr. Thirkel in serious tones, "we need new students here at Caraway. The time has come to expand; these are decisive days in the life of the college. We are at the Rubicon. I want two hundred more students in the freshman class next year."

Mr. Whittle did not understand what this

had to do with him. "I see," he said cautiously, and waited for Dr. Thirkel's next remark; meanwhile he said to himself: "We are at the River Jordan, not at the Rubicon."

"What I want," said Dr. Thirkel, "are some new ideas, to give the students enthusiasm in their work."

He leaned back in his chair, and gave Mr. Whittle a friendly, encouraging look. "How would you like," he began, "to give a course in the history of European-American relations since 1918?"

"I should have to get some lectures together," said Mr. Whittle uncertainly; "I don't know. . . ."

"You'd have the whole summer to prepare," said Dr. Thirkel. "But I should like to announce it in the prospectus."

"The world is coming to an end," said Mr. Whittle meekly, who would have liked to have the summer to enjoy himself.

"That is the sort of thing I mean," said Dr. Thirkel, enthusiastically; "the changing values, and so forth. We might even call the course something of the kind: what do you think?"

He struck the desk with the palm of his hand. "We must keep up with the times. Shall we, perhaps, call it the Enigma of Russia?"

"Why Russia?" asked Mr. Whittle.

Dr. Thirkel declared that he did not understand the Russians.

"There is nothing enigmatic about the Russians," said Mr. Whittle firmly; "they are simply what we call egocentrics. We can learn a great deal about people from the novels that are written about them; and from the Russian novelists we learn that Russians have great qualities of joy, of passion, of sincerity, and courage; and that they are unable to understand anyone else, or even to make themselves clear to one another. That is the only reason it is hard to get along with the Russians."

"Hm," said Dr. Thirkel, who was not really interested in the subject, and who was already thinking about some other courses he wanted to add to the curriculm.

"The British, on the other hand," Mr. Whittle went on happily, "have no trouble explaining themselves; but they do not always tell the truth. Only the Germans are thoroughly honest, as a matter of fact; they say what they mean, and it is so frightful that nobody believes them."

"The atrocities have been overdone," said Dr. Thirkel. "Nobody in Germany believes them."

"The world is starving," said Mr. Whittle. "An entire generation has already been destroyed."

"We must be ready for vast changes," Dr. Thirkel agreed, "and Caraway must lead the way. I might add that the new dining hall, a gift of the alumni, depends upon the enrollment in the freshman class next September. *Ad astra per aspera;* do not fail me, Whittle."

So saying, with a nod, he dismissed the history professor, who remarked as he went out of the door:

"There will be nothing left of us by September."

Dr. Thirkel did not pay any attention to this remark, which would have appeared incomprehensible to him, if he had heard it.

That night after supper Mr. Whittle walked

downtown, to take the air, and to buy himself some aspirin tablets at the drug store. But when he found himself in front of the drug store counters loaded with attractive-looking soaps, candies, electric light bulbs, lamp shades, books, magazines, dolls, toilet articles, and cooking utensils, he suddenly decided to treat himself to a present. What is the use of being frugal any more, he thought; let us enjoy ourselves to the hilt. And so, after changing his mind several times, he finally picked out a hammered brass ash tray and a small leather toilet case for himself, a book of comics for Lucinda, and a large cake of green soap marked Moon-Mist for his wife, and started slowly home.

It was early-dark of a cool spring night; the air was moist and gentle, and filled with the sweet scents of grass and freshly turned earth, asphalt, and chimney smoke. Under the trees which lined the streets with their young leaves, lozenges of coppery light shone out from the windows of houses standing firm and dignified back of their hedges, or half hidden among flowering bushes; the street lamps, each with its own faint halo of

mist around it, made little patterns of light
among the leaves. Mr. Whittle heard the crickets around him on the lawns, the frogs and peep-
ers in the meadows below the town; he heard the
gentle night-drone like a murmur in the air, the
faint call of voices, the windy sound of a car
sweeping along another street. From a porch as
he passed, a woman cried out to someone named
Cyril that it was time to come in; the footsteps
of children pattered on the sidewalk. A dog
barked in the distance; in a house near at hand,
someone was singing.

Oh lovely night; oh lovely night.

Mr. Whittle was not much given to poetry;
but all at once the world seemed very beautiful
to him. He thought of the quiet, dark, sweet-
smelling land, silent under the stars, curving
away from him, shadowy and calm; he thought
of the flat-bottomed prairies, the grass and the
wheat bending in the wind, the hot river valleys,
the slow-flowing rivers. He thought of the lonely
hills, where the air was empty and cold, of the
little lighted towns flung out across the land like
sparks from an engine; he thought of the un-

rimmed forests, of the streams full of trout, of
lakes as big as oceans. America, American
night . . . slow-paced and mountain-high . . .
he thought of all the tiny human voices of earth,
the songs and whispers rising like cricket-sound,
like frog-sound into the vast silence. He thought
of the warm, mortal, small sweetness of life,
which was everywhere. . . .

Must it all end? He did not want to lose it.
There will never be anything like this again, he
thought, so beautiful and so sad, so painful, so
mysterious, and so sweet.

As he turned at the corner, to go down his
street, he saw three little girls walking together
in the light of a street lamp, their arms around
each other's waists. In the faint shine of the light,
and in the dapple of the leaves, he thought that
he recognized Lucinda, and her friends Marian
and Ellen; it seemed to him that they were parad-
ing up and down in front of Ralph Wender's
house, while trying to appear not to do so. Mr.
Whittle stood still for a moment, and watched
them. What a performance, he thought.

The little girls walked slowly up and down,

without ever once looking at the house which interested them so much. "I think *A Night in Paradise* is marvelous" said Marian. "Turhan Bey is so smooth, he gives me goose pimples."

"I think Robert Walker is keen," said Ellen. "I think he's super."

"I know who gives Cinda goose pimples," said Marian in a loud whisper: "R. W."

"Oh heavens," cried Lucinda; "really!"

"He does, too," said Marian. "Doesn't he, Ellen?"

"Pooh," said Lucinda. And overcome with delight and embarrassment, she cried:

"I don't know what you're talking about."

Mr. Whittle continued on his way with a smile. Women, he thought, must manage to get themselves noticed, if they are to be courted. At the same time, a woman cannot admit that anything is of very much importance to her, because she knows that such an admission would put her in jeopardy. She is like Atalanta, who always appeared fully armed and ready for anything, and was only vanquished by her own curiosity. It is unlikely that she would have stopped to pick up the golden apples for any other reason, since she was a sensible girl, and had no use for them.

What is really wonderful, he went on, is that this young Wender, who is nothing but a sticky little boy, will actually be pulled in by all this, and have his curiosity aroused. He already knows perfectly well that Lucinda finds him attractive; for instinct is always sound in such matters. Just the same, being human, he will still be a little doubtful, and want to be reassured. And besides, I am sure that he is already jealous of Mr. Turhan Bey and Mr. Robert Walker, who are irresistible, but not any more so, he thinks, than he would be himself if he were only given the chance. The curious part of it is that he is at least partly right; for the value of a work of art is greatly improved when everyone is talking about it.

How absurd we all are, he thought. As though it matters a hoot what young Mr. Wender thinks about my daughter, considering what is hanging over the entire human race.

And he gave an ironic smile. But a few moments later, as he drew near his own house, he

saw a young couple approaching him, who looked
vaguely familiar. Half seen, under the dark
shadows of the trees, they seemed to him mysterious, and beautiful, and he felt a wave of affection and benevolence toward them. But as they
drew near, they passed beneath a street lamp,
and Mr. Whittle recognized Penelope Andrews
and Marvin Greene; and then they did not seem
beautiful any more.

He heard Penelope give a little laugh, which
sounded innocent and gay. "Oh Marvin," she
exclaimed, "you're a one"; to which Mr. Greene
merely answered:

"Cut it out."

Penelope was not as happy as she sounded;
but Mr. Whittle had no way of knowing it. As
far as he could see, the two young people were in
love with each other; and this astonished him,
for he could not imagine anyone being in love
with Marvin Greene. In choosing a youth of
nineteen, who wore his shirt tails sticking out,
it seemed to him that Penelope was throwing
herself away.

Penelope was also beginning to wonder

whether she was throwing herself away, but for an altogether different reason. She believed that she was in love with Marvin, that she would die without him, and that the summer would be unbearably dull if she did not see him every day; but she had to admit that he had grown somewhat cold to her. She tried to keep her spirits up, but her heart was heavy. "You *are* a one," she said; for she could not think of anything else to say.

Her voice shook a little with disappointment, but Mr. Whittle thought it was emotion that made it tremble.

Just look how she smiles up at him, he thought indignantly; I know that look, I remember it from my youth, from the days when I also was in love. I am sure he does not deserve it; how can she be so stupid? I expected better things of her.

He knew that he was no longer young, because he could not imagine her being in love with Marvin Greene. That is the trouble, he thought, he seems like a child to me, like a schoolboy, or an infant. The truth is, when we think of people being in love, we think only of ourselves; it seems incredible that anyone young enough to be my son should experience such an intimate emotion.

Yes, he thought, I am an old man, that is all there is to it. And with that, the fragrant night air which he had been enjoying no longer seemed to smell so sweet, and the crickets and the frogs seemed to have stopped singing. Those were the sounds of my youth, he thought; and the night air, smelling of honeysuckle and grass, or of lilacs, is also part of a period that is past, a time that is over. It was never just the air itself, however sweet; it was the unknown and beautiful things it suggested, the inexplicable rapture which surrounded me, the hidden joys which lay ahead. They were dreams, and the summer night was like the music which went along with them. Then, the scent of honeysuckle was enough to fill my heart with longing . . . but now if I were to smell it, it would only stir up a few memories, it would not touch my heart. . . .

That is what it is like to grow old: to be untouched by the summer night, by moonlight, by the scent of honeysuckle; to wonder why others should walk hand in hand or with their arms around each other's waist. To be indifferent to the beauty of earth, to be without longing . . .

At the same time, he felt angry and bewildered, because to be forty did not seem to him to be very old.

In a depressed state of mind, he went indoors, and silently handed Amanda the cake of soap he had bought her.

CHAPTER

Five

THE SECOND TIME that Penelope Andrews looked at Mr. Whittle, he took care to look back at her with a cool expression, as though it were the most ordinary thing in the world. But all the time, he could feel that there was something altogether out of the ordinary between them.

It was toward the beginning of class, and he was careful not to glance in her direction again until the hour was nearly over. Then he found her gazing dreamily out of the window, with her back to him; and felt as if he had been cheated out of something.

When he saw her coming up to his desk after class, he was surprised, and told himself that he would have to be wary and businesslike. "Yes, Miss Andrews?" he asked; "did you want to see me?"

Penelope did not know why she had come up, really, for she had nothing important to ask him. She had thought that it would be amusing to give Mr. Whittle another one of her looks; and she had been disappointed when he returned it in such an indifferent manner. Things hadn't gone off as she expected; but at the same time, something told her that was not the end of it by any means. She was piqued, she felt that she had been challenged instead of being the challenger as she had meant to be. Perhaps Mr. Whittle was different from what she had imagined. And suddenly, wanting to be noticed, and feeling — to her surprise — a little uncertain of herself, she decided to go up and speak to him after class.

"Yes, Miss Andrews?"

The trouble was, she didn't have anything to say. She asked him something about Robespierre; and when he answered, she opened her eyes wide at him, and kept her lips parted a little.

Mr. Whittle tried to keep his mind on the French Revolution. She had strangely dark lashes, he thought; and her mouth was quite pretty. "The analogy between Robespierre and George Washington is not exactly — not exactly . . ."

Her skin had a little down on it, like a peach.

"In any case," he said suddenly, in a harsh voice, "no one cares; it is all as dead as a mackerel."

Her parted lips opened wider, and then closed; a look of astonishment appeared in her eyes, which immediately veiled themselves in a smile. "Oh Professor Whittle," she murmured; "you're a one."

I, too, he thought; and smiled somberly back at her. "You don't really care about the French Revolution, do you?" he remarked.

"Well," she said uncertainly, "its very historic, of course. . . ."

Now what was he up to?

"I think," said Mr. Whittle carefully, "that you would rather spend your time with Marvin Greene."

She flushed; the color spread pink and accusing over her cheeks, and all down her neck. "That's my business, isn't it?" she whispered.

"I'm sorry," said Mr. Whittle unhappily. "I was only joking."

Suddenly, to his amazement, her eyes filled with tears. "I think you're horrid," she cried; and turning, rushed from the room.

He half rose from his seat behind the desk, and then sat down again, frowning and uncertain. Good Lord, he thought; good heavens. He felt ashamed, and yet excited in a way; he believed that he had made a fool of himself, and at the same time he felt that there was no longer a wide gulf between them. As he prepared for his next class, he hummed a little tune under his breath. It was the same tune he had heard someone singing the night before, although he had forgotten having heard it. He felt light-hearted, cool, indifferent, and a little shaky.

That afternoon, on his way home, he stopped in to see Miss Euphemia Warren, the instructor in art at the college, who was an old friend of his. He found her studying some sketches which had been made by her pupils, and which she had lined up on a board along one side of the room. Pointing to them, she exclaimed:

"I suppose it is natural for young people to see only what is directly under their noses."

And she added in tragic tones:

"For this I gave up the right to starve in an attic."

Mr. Whittle asked her if she believed that older people could see farther than young ones.

"Certainly," said Miss Warren. "Otherwise I should drown myself."

"Well, then," said Mr. Whittle, "let me ask you this: what do you see ahead?"

"Isms," replied Miss Warren promptly. "I see only isms ahead. I see people forever setting themselves apart because they believe in whorls or in curlicues, or because they only paint with a palette knife, or prefer the color green. Have some tea."

So saying, she went to draw a cupful of water from a small spirit stove which stood bubbling and steaming on her desk.

"Thank you," said Mr. Whittle; "for some reason, it has been a very tiring day."

"I think we shall all die very soon," he added after a moment.

"Shall we?" asked Miss Warren. "I only wonder that it hasn't happened long ago."

"We didn't have the means," explained Mr. Whittle. "But now that we have found out how . . ."

"It's all one to me," said Miss Warren calmly. "I only hope we make a good job of it."

Munching a cracker, and dipping it into her tea from time to time, she remarked between mouthfuls:

"I believe that I am on the track of the true meaning of form in the abstract sense."

And she went on to explain her theory to him. "Design," she said, "exists in the universe, and in the mind. It is only necessary to relate the two. The design of the atom is: and the way we see it, is the way it is. Whatever we see, exists in the form in which we see it, neither more nor less; and not because we see it. If we did not see it, it would still exist, but there would be no correlation. Do I make myself clear?"

Mr. Whittle did not answer directly. Instead, he asked:

"What is the name of this theory, Euphemia?"

"Mutualism," said Miss Warren. "All the rest is folderol."

Nobody seems to care a fiddle for the end of the world, thought Mr. Whittle as he went home.

On his way, he stopped off a minute at the Country Club, to pick up Mr. Blaney, who was usually there at this hour of the day, for business reasons. The banker was at the bar with several friends and acquaintances, and Mr. Whittle joined him there. "I'm ready any time you are, Alfred," he said.

Mr. Blaney was not a drinking man; but he had not felt like himself ever since his visit to the Whittles the week before. Now as he drove Mr. Whittle home through the late afternoon, he was in a mellow mood due to his having had several more drinks than he was accustomed to. And he felt that he ought to give Mr. Whittle some good advice, that he ought to tell him something that he had found out for himself, and that he didn't think Mr. Whittle realized.

60

"I want to tell you something," he said. "There's something you don't know. You don't know what a very unusual wife you've got."

He frowned, and hit the steering wheel with the palm of his hand. "No sir," he said; "your wife is an unusual woman."

Mr. Whittle was pleased to think that Mr. Blaney admired his wife, but he did not know what to say. "That's right," he agreed; "she is." And he murmured affectionately:

"Amanda."

But he could not imagine why Mr. Blaney felt obliged to refer to her at this moment.

Mr. Blaney himself could not explain it. His mind was filled with a great many serious thoughts, none of which was clear enough to put into words. He felt that he was on the edge of an important explanation of something, the exact nature of which escaped him.

"I've been married fifteen years," he said finally, "to a good woman. The backbone of the country. . . . Where would we be without it?"

Leaning forward against the steering wheel,

he peered around into Mr. Whittle's face, and laid one hand on his knee in a questioning way.

"Hey?" he asked.

"Look where you're going, Alfred," said Mr. Whittle.

Mr. Blaney straightened up with dignity, and focused his eyes upon the road ahead. "Don't worry," he said; "I'll get you home. I want to live just as much as you do."

Do I? thought Mr. Whittle gently to himself. He thought about his life, its simple, prosy pattern, the few surprises, the few pleasures he could look forward to, the many indignities and humiliations he had endured. He thought of all the courses in history he would have to teach, year after year, all the meals he would have to eat, all the errands he would have to do; he thought of the long, cold winters with their icy winds, when he was busy with the furnace day and night, the short hot summers with their mosquitoes and thunderstorms . . . unchanging days, unchanging years, with only a moment stolen here and there for a walk in the evening, for the sound of a song . . . the slow decay of life in him and around him. . . .

Yes, he thought with surprise, I want to live, I am jealous of every moment that I might miss if I were not here.

The image of Penelope Andrews appeared suddenly in his mind; dressed in a tight-fitting sweater, she came toward him with a voluptuous motion, and slightly parted lips. Mr. Whittle was shocked, and glanced sideways at Mr. Blaney in embarrassment. But Mr. Blaney was thinking his own thoughts, and did not appear to notice him.

"My mother brought me up to respect womanhood," said Mr. Blaney. "She wouldn't let my father smoke a cigar in the house, and she wore her collar right up to her chin. It had whalebone in it."

He began to sing, throwing back his head, and keeping time with one hand,

> *"I hear those angel voices calling*
> *Old Black Joe."*

"Alfred!" exclaimed Mr. Whittle, as an approaching sedan swerved out of the way just in time to avoid a collision.

"Don't worry," said Mr. Blaney. "I'll get you home."

"You nearly hit that car," said Mr. Whittle.

"I wouldn't say that," said Mr. Blaney.

He was silent for a moment. Then, "I wish my mother were alive," he said suddenly. "She was the backbone of the country."

And although that was all he said, Mr. Whittle understood him, his cloudy thoughts somehow made themselves clear without any more words. We knew where we were then, he seemed to say, because they told us. They were old and wise and right, just, virtuous, and implacable; they broke our hearts, they protected us from folly, they saved us from the results of being human. No one tells us any more, we are supposed to know it all for ourselves. . . . Only, so much has happened, and God is not at our elbow, the way He used to be. Men bring their cigars into the house, and children are not respectful. . . . Mother would have changed all that. She would have kept her home in

whalebone, no matter what happened outside. . . .

And who knows? — perhaps in that case the
world would not have ended so soon. If we had
been more virtuous, and more severe — less willing to put up with evil, for the sake of peace and
comfort, less willing to look away from wrong,
and call it minding our own business . . .

"Gone are the days," sang Mr. Blaney, and
waved a friendly greeting to the policeman at
the corner of Elm and Clark.

"It's too late now," he said.

But he wasn't thinking about the world, or
even about his mother any more. He was thinking about Amanda Whittle, and what it would
have been like with her — instead of Ruth. Not
to change all his life, of course — not to change
Ellen for Lucinda, or any of the other things
. . . not to be that poor thing, Whittle, himself. But to come into a room — his own room,
say — and to see Amanda there . . . Amanda,
with her mouse-brown hair, and her gentle,
pretty ways . . . to know that she belonged
there, that it was all for him, the sigh, the down-

cast look, the soft encircling arms . . . all for him. Just once, he thought, with her . . . just once, before he got to be an old man, and life was over and done with — before there was nothing left to remember, even, except the bank, and Ruth . . .

Mr. Whittle did not share in these thoughts with Mr. Blaney, which was a fortunate thing. He nodded his head soberly.

"Yes, Alfred," he said; "it's too late now."

C H A P T E R

Six

FAMILIES usually meet at meals, and only rarely at other times. A family sits down to dinner, its members draw closer to one another, for a moment they have an interest in common: what is there to eat? For a moment, the solitude which hides one from another is lightened, and they enjoy a sense of communion in the soup, meat, and vegetables. From this communion, the spirit still holds back, lonely, and unreconciled.

The Whittles sat at the dinner table in accustomed silence. After fourteen years of marriage, Mr. Whittle no longer felt obliged to tell his wife everything that had happened to him during the day, but this was not to say that he was lacking in affection or interest. He was happy to hear about anything that had occurred in the household during his absence; he was glad to

hear that the plumber had come as he had prom-
ised, or that there were still eight quarts of vegetables in the cellar, left over from what Amanda
had put up the year before. And he clucked with
sympathy when he learned that the laundress
had burned a hole in one of the sheets. But as
for what he himself had been doing, it seemed
hardly worth talking about.

Lucinda, too, was silent; she scarcely knew
where she was. In her dreamy mind, she relived
the last excursion down the street with her
friends, Marian and Ellen, and smiled from time
to time, or sighed for no apparent reason.

Amanda looked at Mr. Whittle with a little
puzzled pucker between her eyes. He seemed so
unusually silent, even for him; and his thoughts,
to judge by the secret, folded-in look on his face,
were further away than ever. Perhaps he had
been working too hard; or else it could be the
spring, and the change of weather. "Do you feel
all right, dear?" she asked.

"Eh?" he said, rousing himself; "yes, certainly. Why?"

And he looked around the table in a brisk manner.

Meeting her father's mild, inquiring eye, Lucinda drew into herself, and stared down at her plate. Well, that was the trouble; people were always interfering with her. And she tried to shut out both her parents from her dream in which, dressed in a beautiful dirndl skirt and ruffled blouse, she was being escorted to the drug store by Mr. Wender for a cherry-cola with ice cream, while Ellen and Marian looked on enviously from across the street. Pardon me, she murmured in a delicious voice; Ralph and I wish to be alone.

"Lucinda," said her mother, "eat your peas."

"Oh, heck," said Lucinda.

Amanda looked tenderly and with sympathy at her husband. The final examinations were coming soon, and that always meant more work for the teachers.

"Anything new?" she asked.

Mr. Whittle shook his head. "I picked up Alfred at the club," he remarked; "he's a dreadful

driver. And I stopped off to see Euphemia Warren. . . ."

His face grew suddenly secretive and smooth,
and his eyes veiled themselves in indifference. He
had been going backwards through the day, and
he had got to Penelope. . . .

"That's all," he said.

He didn't quite know why he wanted to keep
Penelope a secret. But it was really to save himself from having to decide anything about her.
Nothing could happen as long as nobody knew;
nothing could happen to him or to Amanda as
long as nobody said anything. Words were like
that, they started things up, they started things
happening; after something had been put into
words, it was there, even if it hadn't been there
before. And then something had to be done about
it; and in any case, there was a situation.

Nothing, absolutely nothing had happened;
but if he said "I spoke to a girl named Penelope
Andrews," he would be bringing her into his
home, and he would never be able to get her out
again. Not completely. It was like throwing a

pebble into a pond; the ripples died down after a while, but the pebble was still there, in the pond.

Amanda noticed the withdrawal, the tight, closed look; and her heart made a sudden, slight pause in her breast. There's something he isn't telling me, she thought; there's something he doesn't want to talk about.

And with a little feeling of panic, she stared at the table, to hide her eyes.

There were so many things it could be: unpleasantness at the college, trouble with Dr. Thirkel . . . he might even have been asked to resign. . . .

But that was unthinkable; and how could she ever bear to tell her parents? She knew what they would say: we expected it right along, it doesn't surprise us in the least, but you can count on us to help you, if necessary.

Never, she thought hotly; never in this world. And she began to figure out how she could do without a laundress, and what she could give up until Robert found another position. Because

he would, of course; he was such a good teacher,
everybody said. . . .

"The President has asked me to take another
course next season," said Mr. Whittle. "I shall
have to get some notes together very soon. . . ."

Relief made her, for a moment, feel almost
weak. "What a pity," she murmured. Well, that
was probably it; he hadn't wanted to talk about
it.

She felt humble, and ashamed of herself. Poor
Robert, she thought; he works so hard, and what
does he get out of it? Just this little badly-run
home, and an extravagant wife. I don't really
need a laundress; other women do their own laun-
dry, even the sheets and the towels. Or maybe I
could send the sheets out. . . . Maybe I ought
to sell the car, Robert hardly uses it at all, except in winter, but then of course in winter we
wouldn't have it . . . and sometimes in summer
it's nice to get away to the lake or somewhere. . . . Perhaps we ought to have some
people in to dinner. Euphemia Warren, Robert
likes her even though I don't, but then, I
hardly know her; and Dr. Thirkel. If he'd come;

but it might seem as though we were pushing ourselves. . . .

"Anyway," she declared, "I can do without lunch after this, and that will save quite a good deal."

"Why should you do without lunch?" asked Mr. Whittle.

"I'm sure we're spending too much money," she said. "We ought to save a lot more than we do. And anyway, I'm getting fat."

"You're nothing of the kind," said Mr. Whittle. "It isn't good for you to diet; you always catch a cold.

"Besides," he added, "I like you the way you are. And so does Alfred."

Amanda looked up in surprise. Alfred? Alfred Blaney? Had he really said something like that? It was the last thing in the world she expected.

"You just made that up," she said, "so I'd fall for it."

"He considers you a very unusual woman," said Mr. Whittle. "He told me so."

"Oh, pooh," said Amanda. Unusual, indeed.

That was nothing to be so pleased about. A midget was unusual, and so was a two-headed calf. "What's so unusual about me?" she asked.

Frowning, she looked down at her waist, which, free and uncorseted, was round, firm, and not at all too fat. "I ought to take off at least five pounds," she said.

"You were in bed two weeks the last time," Mr. Whittle reminded her. "With pneumonia."

"It wasn't pneumonia," said Amanda; "it was bronchitis. Everybody had it. It was an epidemic."

Mr. Whittle sighed. It was never any good arguing with Amanda. She said things out of habit, or to see how they would sound; and then she talked herself into them.

"What did Alfred really say?" she asked, smoothing out her skirt over her lap.

Mr. Whittle looked at his wife quietly; he tried to see her as Mr. Blaney did. But Mr. Blaney only saw her now and then, and Mr. Whittle saw her every day. There was too much mixed up in it, too many years of being together, of living in the same house, the same room . . . too much intimacy, and even too much affection. It is the strangeness of people, he thought, that stirs and wounds us; when we are young, the whole world is there to be explored. Still, to Mr. Blaney, Amanda was as unexplored as Africa.

Supposing she were to leave me, he thought; to die; or to go away on a trip. Or simply to grow tired of me. . . .

At once a feeling of intense anxiety, and even of grief, seized hold of him. He realized that he could not live without her; and imagining himself alone and deserted, uttered a soundless groan.

It was his own fault; he had allowed all the strangeness to go out of their lives; he had let himself become as ordinary to her as an old shoe. And so, when Alfred said . . . because Alfred was a stranger . . .

She sat looking at him, and smiling gently; she was feeling sorry for him again. I'm not a very good wife, really, she thought; I'm not very attractive or interesting; I might as well admit it.

If there were only something she could do. . . .

"Would you like to go somewhere tonight?" she asked shyly. She had nothing in mind, but it would be nice to do something together, even if they only went to a movie.

"There's a super movie at the Fox-Rivertown," declared Lucinda. "It's about this person who thinks he murdered somebody but he isn't sure, and there's a lot of shooting and everything. It's super."

Mr. and Mrs. Whittle exchanged a look of doubt. "What's at the Orpheum, dear?" asked Mrs. Whittle.

"Oh, something droopy," said Lucinda. "You know — love, and things like that."

By love, she meant grown-up people kissing each other, which made her feel embarrassed and ashamed. What she felt for Ralph Wender was no more meaty than a butterfly; and that was the way things ought to be. On the screen, she liked Westerns, or people falling downstairs.

The Whittles went to the Orpheum; they sat side by side in the dark, listened to the music, and watched the hero and heroine, ten feet high, meet, insult each other, fall in love, marry, lose each other, and finally make up again. It was all very improbable, but it had cost several million dollars. "I love you," said the hero, while the music played in the background, "because I can see the soul of the prairies in your eyes." He was supposed to be a rough lout, and very good with his fists; but he was handsome, and everybody loved him, and he expressed himself from time to time in poetry.

Mr. and Mrs. Whittle held hands together where nobody could see them. And for a moment, lulled by the darkness and the music, watching the grief and joy of others, which they were not obliged to share, but which reminded them somehow of their own, they felt young again, and full of vague hopes and gentle dreams. Mr. Whittle looked at his wife's profile in the semidarkness; and she seemed like a stranger, secretive and provocative; he felt excited to think that she belonged to him, and fondly pressed her hand. We must do this more often, he thought.

The faces of the actor and actress, enlarged

to gigantic size, moved together in a final embrace, and the picture was over. Mr. and Mrs. Whittle, followed by Lucinda, came out into the lobby, and blinked in the light. "Well," said Mr. Whittle, clearing his throat.

"It was definitely corny," said Lucinda.

At that moment, as they started to leave the theater, Mr. Whittle saw Penelope Andrews standing at one end of the lobby, in a group of young women. He hoped he would not have to speak to her, but when she turned, suddenly, and saw him, she flushed a bright color, and murmured in a confused way:

"Oh . . . hello."

"Good evening," said Mr. Whittle, and passed by with his wife.

Followed by Lucinda, Mr. and Mrs. Whittle walked along the street in silence. Presently Amanda said, in a casual tone:

"Who was that?"

"Who?" asked Mr. Whittle.

"The girl you spoke to," said Amanda.

Mr. Whittle replied that it was just a girl in one of his classes. . . .

"I see," said Amanda. She was silent a moment. Then:

"Why did she blush when she saw you?"

Mr. Whittle's heart sank. "I can't imagine," he murmured. And he began to whistle a tune under his breath.

"It was strange," said Amanda. "She was quite a pretty girl."

She looked back, to make sure that Lucinda was following them. "What was her name?" she asked.

"I believe she is a Miss Andrews," said Mr. Whittle indifferently.

"So you know her," said Amanda.

"I told you," said Mr. Whittle; "she is in my class. . . ."

"It's very strange you never spoke of her," said Amanda. And she added, after a moment:

"Why would she blush like that?"

Her voice was light and cool, but Mr. Whittle was not fooled by it. So now the whole evening was spoiled, he thought; but he did not know what to do about it. "Shall we stop in somewhere for a soda?" he asked hopefully.

"I don't believe I want any, thank you," said Amanda.

At once they both heard a wail from behind them. "Oh Mommy!" cried Lucinda. After having to sit through all that corny love-making . . . Really, she thought, parents could be such drips. . . .

"You two go ahead, if you like," said Amanda. "I'll go on home."

That suited Lucinda even better, but not Mr. Whittle. "We'll all go home," he said; "that's probably more sensible, anyhow."

They walked the rest of the way to their car in silence. The still night hung over Rivertown, the stars shone high up in the sky, small and misty above the empty streets; a cold wind blew in from across the river, bringing with it the damp river-smell. Amanda thought of the young girl in the lobby; she might have been eighteen, she could hardly have been more than twenty. She had been with a number of other young people; one of them might have been teasing her. . . .

She stole a glance at her husband. There he

was, middle-aged and weary . . . he was certainly no Lochinvar. Or was it Lochinvar she meant? Well, no matter, it was something like that; Romeo, perhaps. Not to a twenty-year-old. Poor Robert.

Still, the girl had looked right at him . . . but perhaps she had only imagined it. They had had such a good time together at the movie. . . .

She began to feel sorry that she had not gone to the drug store for a soda. But it would never do to admit it.

"It's late," she explained to Lucinda. "You've got school tomorrow."

"It was a good picture," she said to her husband. "I enjoyed it. Thank you."

Even if she was wrong, that was as far as she would go.

CHAPTER

Seven

For several days after that, nothing occurred of serious interest to the Whittles. Then Mr. Whittle gave his annual lecture to the ladies of the St. Vincent Club, affiliated for this occasion with the Literary and Historical Society of Rivertown, and the Ladies' Auxiliary of the Clark Street Church. Some eighty ladies attended the lecture, including Miss Euphemia Warren, and Mrs. Theodore Andrews, the mother of Penelope Andrews.

Standing on a slightly raised platform in the basement auditorium of the Clark Street Church, Mr. Whittle outlined to his hearers the rise and fall of nations from the beginning of time. But time itself, he declared, was something that nobody was able to understand: it was like a rainbow which could only be seen from one direction, and when you got to it, there was nothing there.

"For millions of years," he said, "there existed here upon this earth reptilian forms which no human eye was ever destined to see. The pterodactyl, the dinosaur, roamed the antediluvial plain, and flapped through the steamy air, either in snake-like silence, or with cries and roars which the mind cannot even imagine. Man himself is a new-comer; the dawn of humankind dates back no more than five hundred thousand years.

"Ten thousand years ago, this continent was inhabited by a race of men of which very little is actually known. They hunted the bison, the camel, the woolly mammoth, and the mastodon, and killed them with slender spears tipped with flint. These men had fire; and they must have had a language of a sort, for they used the skins of animals to clothe themselves against the cold. In other words, they were capable of abstract thought. We have been unable to find any of their bones; but we have found their flints, and traces of their campfires hidden beneath the detritus of the great glaciers. In four hundred and ninety thousand years, then, it seems that man had learned something; but not very much.

"Five thousand years later, in the Mediterranean basin, legend tells us of cities of mud and stone, which perished in volcanic upheavals or beneath the waves of the Great Flood. Thereafter, we come to history itself, of which the earliest hieroglyphs give us only the record of endless wars. Thus, from the hunter in his cave, we come after many thousands of years to the quarrels of nations, and the rise of empires.

"There are two ways of measuring time: by its duration, or by its sequence. That is to say, by how long it takes, or by what happens in it. The life-span of an elephant is well over a hundred years, that of the ephemera less than a day. Nevertheless in each case that span of time is all there is, and represents an entire experience; and can therefore be said to be equal, and the same.

"During these later centuries, history has seemed to accelerate. Let me give you an example. The civilization of Egypt was not very much different from that of Rome. It took two thousand years for Rome to rise, and Thebes to decline; but less than two hundred to build the city of Chicago on the site of a buffalo wallow.

"Let me give you another example. Five hundred years ago, men still lit their fires with flint and tinder; their weapons were still the spear and the bow, the axe and the knife. Aspirin and rubber were undreamed of; the world was generally believed to be flat.

"And in the last fifty years, man has learned to fly!

"What extraordinary things have happened in the span of our single lifetime. Electricity alone has changed the world, it has conquered darkness and space. Man moves with the speed of sound; with a drop of medicine he destroys the most dreaded bacteria; he changes glass into cloth, creates new fruits and flowers, and watches pictures which move and speak in such a way as to give an illusion of reality. He talks, in less than a minute, to the most distant parts of the globe, where the only difficulty is that he does not understand the language. And in learning, at last, to split the atom, he has discovered a way to blow up not only himself, but the entire planet as well.

"Can we still believe, then, that time can be measured by duration alone? Or that the last one hundred years of our existence are not more multifold — since so much more has happened in them — than all the years which have gone before?

"I am inclined to believe that we cannot; I believe that we must measure time by how much is packed into it, and that we have come to the end of human time.

"Having learned to blow ourselves up, we shall certainly do so. In our quarrels to see who is to rule this planet, we shall destroy it; we shall destroy our enemies and ourselves at the same time. We shall all go up in one vast explosion, in one great white light, along with everything

that we have learned, or even thought about —
in short, along with the entire history of humanity. In all the universe, there will be no one left
to know what Man was, what he looked like, or
how he lived.

"I am convinced that this is our destiny; I see
no way to avoid it, and I do not expect that we
shall ever meet again. I thank you."

At the end of this extraordinary speech, the
ladies sat as if stunned. Then they got up, and
several indignant remarks were exchanged.
"That is not my idea of a constructive talk,"
said the president of the St. Vincent Club. And
the treasurer of the Ladies' Auxiliary declared:
"I haven't the faintest inkling of what it was all
about."

"To say that there were men alive five hundred thousand years ago," remarked one lady,
"is nonsense. God created Adam and Eve in the
Garden of Eden; and then there was Sodom and
Gomorrah. I'd rather believe in the Bible than
in what I've heard here today."

"In any case," declared another lady, "I think
it's a shame to say that we are going to destroy

ourselves. I, for one, haven't the least intention of doing anything of the kind. We need moral leadership in the world, optimism, and courage. I am shocked at Professor Whittle, and I feel very sorry for his wife."

During all this, Euphemia Warren came up to Mr. Whittle and silently pressed his hand. "What you said," she declared, "interests me very much; and I admire your courage in saying it. I agree with you: we must correlate what is with what we see. Come to tea some day, and I will show you some studies I have done in the field of abstract design."

Mr. Whittle gathered his papers together and turned to leave the room. He felt empty and tired, but satisfied that he had said the right thing. It is impossible to get anybody to think seriously about the end of the world, he thought, except during a thunderstorm. Either you believe in God, or you do not; but in either case, there is only one thing to do: for all men, everywhere, to work for the good of all — which is extremely unlikely, in any event.

As he was going out of the door, a lady stopped

him, and remarked in a friendly way: "Professor Whittle, I am so glad to have heard your little talk, because my daughter has spoken of you so often."

"Thank you," said Mr. Whittle. And he hesitated, looking at her with one eyebrow raised, as though to say Do I know you?

With an encouraging smile, the lady added:

"My daughter is in one of your classes. I am Mrs. Andrews . . . my daughter is Penelope Andrews."

"Yes indeed," said Mr. Whittle automatically. He was surprised; and he looked carefully at Mrs. Andrews, as though to take her all in at a single glance. Yes, he could see a certain resemblance . . . but she was not as good-looking as her daughter. She was simply a middle-aged woman. . . . And forgetting that he had just delivered a lecture on the meaning of time, he thought to himself, How can a handful of years make such a difference?

"Your daughter is in History IV," said Mr. Whittle; "I believe she is doing very well."

Mrs. Andrews nodded. "Yes," she said. And

she added: "It was such an interesting lecture."

"Thank you," said Mr. Whittle again; and with a polite bow, turned and left the room.

But on his way home, he suddenly stood still, frowned, and pursed up his mouth in a low whistle. What was it Mrs. Andrews had said? "My daughter has spoken of you so often. . . ."

Obviously, she had made that up on the spur of the moment; it was out of the question. But then — why should she have said it at all? To put him at his ease? He had not been in the least embarrassed. Or to establish a closer tie between them? That was unlikely . . . there was no need for it. . . .

Well, then — perhaps she had not made it up after all. It was not altogether out of the question, of course.

So Penepole had spoken of him, at home.

But why had she done so? That was what puzzled him; for their worlds were as far apart as hawk and ant. . . .

It was an uncomfortable simile; which was he, ant or hawk? Neither one, as a matter of fact.

It was more sensible to say merely that she was a young girl with nothing more in her head than a young girl's usual thoughts.

But suddenly it seemed to him that he saw her there beside him, walking along under the trees with their gently rustling leaves. And he seemed to hear her say: "Oh, you . . . you're a one."

At this, he suddenly felt cold, his head seemed to whirl, and he smiled shyly down at the pavement, at his feet. Was it really possible? He remembered that she had blushed, when she had seen him. . . .

My dear child, he said to her in his mind, in a fatherly way; my dear child. . . .

But then he could not think of anything more to say. After all, he must not take things for granted here; perhaps she was really interested in history after all. At the same time, he had to admit that it was not very likely.

He wondered what she could have said about him to her parents. But that was something really difficult to imagine. And in the imagined presence of these unknown parents, who were his

91

own age, or very nearly, but who nevertheless seemed older to him, he felt embarrassed and uncomfortable. I assure you, he said to them in earnest tones, I am not interested in your daughter simply because she is young and attractive. . . . After all, I have some sense; I am not an idiot, exactly.

Eight

BUT EVENTS now began to move more swiftly.

Next morning, as Amanda was doing her shopping at the market, she ran into Mrs. Burkit, the wife of the minister of the Clark Street Church. Mrs. Burkit seemed somewhat cool; nevertheless, surrounded by cans of peaches and asparagus, jars of coffee and peanut butter, jellies, prepared noodles, and packages of dried cereal, the two ladies, each pushing before her a wire cart on wheels, discussed with an appearance of politeness the difficulties of housekeeping, the late spring, the coming summer, and the high price of everything.

"I cannot keep Lucinda in dresses any more," said Amanda; "she grows out of them so fast." Bending over, she peered doubtfully at a small jar of spaghetti with tomato sauce. "Starch," she said, with a sigh.

"You can't make them look nice," said Mrs. Burkit, "no matter what you do." And she gave a snort, to show what she thought about the whole question.

"The way that children grow up nowadays," she remarked, "is a scandal. Six feet high, every one of them. I don't know what the world is coming to."

However, this seemed to remind her of something. "That reminds me," she said; and gave her little cart a push toward the cereals. "Your husband made some very strange remarks yesterday. We ladies were surprised, to put it mildly."

Amanda straightened up, and looked at Mrs. Burkit questioningly. Strange remarks? Of course, Robert hadn't shown her his lecture — but then, he never did. What could he have said? She felt a little tremor of anxiety.

"Yes?" she murmured, waiting for the worst.

"All this about the end of the world," said

Mrs. Burkit severely; "really, Mrs. Whittle!"

Oh Lord, thought Amanda.

"It isn't as though Professor Whittle spoke
of it in a religious way," Mrs. Burkit went
on; "quite the contrary. Quite, quite the contrary!"

"Robert is very anxious," said Amanda loyally, "for the future of humanity."

"He should go to church more often," said
Mrs. Burkit. "He should seek God; that would
allay his anxiety."

"But you see," said Amanda, "he thinks —
that we ourselves. . . ."

Her voice trailed off uncertainly. She was always a little confused between God and Mr.
Whittle.

"My husband," declared Mrs. Burkit, mov-
ing down toward the lemon pop and ginger ale,
"was surprised and shocked at Professor Whittle's statements. He called them Cynicism, or
worse; but I will spare you the full gist of his
remarks. Surely you are too good a church-goer
yourself, Mrs. Whittle, to believe that man

came into being without God's help, like a nectarine."

"I am sure," said Amanda unhappily, "that Robert never meant that man came into being without God's help, Mrs. Burkit."

The minister's wife gave a loud sniff through her nose. "You should have heard him," she said.

She dug her strong, thin fingers into a melon, and then lifted it doubtfully to her nose. "Humph," she remarked.

"Still," she said, "that's not the point. It is not the past, but the present which is a matter of concern to Dr. Burkit. He is the shepherd of his flock; the souls of two hundred and sixty-two Christians, not including unbaptized infants, are in his charge. He is responsible for them."

Amanda felt depressed; and she felt a little frightened. In the dry tones of Mrs. Burkit's voice, she heard the moral judgment of an older generation; and in Mrs. Burkit's bright, sharp, and unrelenting eye she saw the condemnation of a virtuous community. She felt like a little girl again, shamefaced, and in the wrong. "I am sure Robert did not mean anything sacrilegious," she murmured weakly.

"He meant what he said," snapped Mrs. Burkit; "he said the world would be destroyed by man, not God. There were no two ways about it, so far as I could see."

Upright, stern, and in a triumphant mood, she approached the cashier. "No, Mrs. Whittle," she said; "it will be a long time before your husband is asked to speak at the Clark Street Church again."

Amanda went home in a state of nerves, and for the rest of the day tried to forget her troubles in hard work. She scrubbed the upstairs and downstairs floors, cleaned out the ice-box, washed the bed-spread on Lucinda's bed and set it out to dry, and cleaned out three closets. But all the time she was impatient, and rebellious. For eight long years she had worked to make a place for herself and her family in Rivertown: eight years of politeness and good works, eight years of a clean house and a friendly word with the neighbors, of freshly starched dresses for Lucinda, and contributions to the Community Chest, and the Girl Scouts. And now Robert had thrown it all away — standing there on his lecture platform, like a puffed-up frog. . . . It was all for nothing, all her work. . . .

Oh, damn him anyway, she thought.

The Whittles were in jeopardy, and she knew it. For she knew the sort of community in which she lived . . . actually, it was the only kind of community she did know. People took to you and respected you because you were like themselves — because you believed what they believed, and spoke the same language. When you acted in a way they didn't understand, or said things they didn't like, they rejected you; they turned away when you passed them on the street, and looked uncomfortable when they met you. A man had no right to say everything he thought, not when he was married, and had a wife and daughter to consider. The least he could do was to keep his ideas to himself.

At five o'clock Mr. Whittle returned from the college in a relaxed frame of mind. The day had been warm, and he was tired; it seemed to him that there were a great many people in the world, and that they were all made of something hard and impenetrable, like glass, or stone. He found his wife with a dusty face, down on her knees, stubbornly scrubbing the kitchen floor. "Well," he said uncertainly; "do you have to do that?"

"Somebody has to," she replied shortly.

Mr. Whittle's face grew longer, and seemed to sag a little. He knew that Amanda was in a temper, that there was something in the wind; and he went quietly into his study, and shut the door. A moment later it was flung open, and Mrs. Whittle appeared on the threshold, with blazing eyes.

"Do you think that's very polite?" she demanded; "to slam the door in my face?"

Mr. Whittle swallowed, as one does going down too rapidly in an elevator. "I didn't slam the door," he said. "I'm sorry."

And he added, half under his breath:

"I've had a hard day."

"Oh yes," said Mrs. Whittle sarcastically; "sitting down. . . . I wish just once you could do half of what I have to do every day of my life. Cooking, cleaning, making beds. . . ."

"Can't Lucinda help you?" asked Mr. Whittle.

"Lucinda goes to school," replied his wife in exasperated tones; "or had you forgotten? I suppose you want the child to have no time to herself at all."

"Well," said Mr. Whittle, "if you'd like me to do anything. . . ."

"It's all done," said Mrs. Whittle coldly. She stood staring at him in smoldering resentment. "The trouble with you is," she said, "you think nobody has anything to do but yourself."

"That isn't true," said Mr. Whittle wearily. "I realize that you work very hard."

"So that you can have a comfortable home," said Mrs. Whittle.

"Why, yes," said Mr. Whittle; but at the same time he began to feel bewildered, and heavy-hearted. "I work, too," he said mildly. "For whom do you think I do all this?"

And he made a vague gesture toward his desk, piled high with books and papers.

"Lucinda works all day long in school," said Mrs. Whittle. "I suppose you don't want her to get a single breath of air."

"I only meant . . ." began Mr. Whittle.

Mrs. Whittle let out a snort, not unlike Mrs. Burkit. "Why don't you make some sense?" she asked.

Mr. Whittle's eyes narrowed; he slowly clenched and unclenched his fist. "Look," he said quietly; "suppose you tell me what you're so angry about?"

"I wouldn't dream of it," said Mrs. Whittle, with a scornful laugh. "What makes you think I'm angry! Just because *you* come home in a fury, and go into your room and slam the door. . . ."

"I didn't slam the door," said Mr. Whittle.

"But just the same," Mrs. Whittle continued, "it's pretty discouraging to work and slave to give you a good home, and then have you do the kind of things you do."

"What kind of things?" asked Mr. Whittle.

"You know very well what kind of things,"

said Mrs. Whittle. "You've made a fine failure of yourself, I must say."

Mr. Whittle looked out of his study window to where the little yard between his house and his neighbor's lay in the warm shadow of late afternoon. A fly droned against the screen; he could hear the faint shouts of children down the street. A small breeze blew in through the window, and stirred the papers on his desk; it smelled of grass, and oil from the garage. Mr. Whittle felt very weary, and a little angry.

"I didn't realize I was such a failure," he said coldly.

"Oh, why don't you grow up?" cried Mrs. Whittle.

"Really!" exclaimed Mr. Whittle. "I suppose you think *you're* acting in a grown-up way," he demanded.

"I certainly am," said Mrs. Whittle. And with moist eyes, she added:

"Still, if you don't like the way I act, perhaps I can find somewhere else to go."

"Yes?" asked Mr. Whittle. "Where?"

Mrs. Whittle had simply intended going into

another room. But at her husband's query, she changed her mind.

"I guess Lucinda and I can find a place to live," she said, "seeing that we're not wanted here."

"Just a minute," said Mr. Whittle. "I never said . . ."

"You meant it, though," said Mrs. Whittle, while her eyes filled. "You wish you were free; you said so yourself. You hate having a family."

"Don't be ridiculous," said Mr. Whittle sharply.

"I am not ridiculous," said Mrs. Whittle.

"I never said anything of the sort," said Mr. Whittle.

"You don't have to say it," declared Mrs. Whittle; "it's perfectly clear; you hate me. Why don't you admit it? Why do you lie about it?"

"Oh, damn it," said Mr. Whittle.

"Kindly keep your voice down," cried Mrs. Whittle; "or do you want everybody to know what kind of a man you are? Well, there's no use going on this way: we don't get along any more, that's all. You'll be better off without me;

103

you know it, but you're just too cowardly to say so. Don't worry; I'll manage. I'll get a job somewhere, and take Lucinda off your hands, as long as you hate us both so much. And you can go on and make a fool of yourself to your heart's content. Everybody is making fun of you. They think you're absurd. It's just too bad you haven't sense enough to see it."

And with a loud wail, she turned, and bolted from the room, slamming the door behind her. A few minutes later, Mr. Whittle rose from his chair and, taking his hat in a dazed way, left the house.

Upstairs, Mrs. Whittle was weeping into her pillow. She could no longer remember any of the things she had said; but she felt that she had been absolutely right. Everything was over between them . . . at least, until Mr. Whittle apologized.

CHAPTER

Nine

THE SLANTING SHADOWS of late afternoon had
given way to the smoky blue of evening, which
in turn had deepened into night. Mr. Whittle
plodded wearily along the River Road; he could
hear the sound of the river below him, in the
dark; and he could see the town lights ahead of
him. The air around him was damp, and heavy
with the smell of earth, of rotted logs, and ferns.
It was cold in the hollows; the moon, at the half,
rode high overhead in the western sky, bright as
a coin; but it was hidden from Mr. Whittle by
the trees.

He had been walking a long while out into the
country and back, and his legs were tired; but
he had not regained his peace of mind. This was
not the first quarrel he had had with Amanda,
but for some reason it seemed to him the most de-

cisive and unreasonable. He could not forget that she had called him absurd, and that she had said that everybody thought so. He did not believe that everybody thought so; and he did not think she had any right to speak to him like that.

Very well: she thought him absurd. And he had made a failure of himself, too. "Look," he said fiercely into the darkness; "who has got the benefit of all my work? I suppose you would be a success without me?"

He felt justified, and outraged; and heavy-hearted because it had all come to this, after fourteen years. It was clear that Amanda had expressed her true feelings, and that she no longer loved him. All right, then he would go on without her, and tell people the truth as he saw it, which was just what he had done that morning, in front of the Literary and Historical Society. Let her leave him, if he was such a failure then.

He did not really believe that she would leave him, for he knew that she was devoted to her home, and that she was not interested in anyone else. At the same time, he felt that something had gone out of their lives forever; and he could not help feeling lonely and deprived, and in need of consolation and affection.

In this unhappy state of mind, he found himself at the outskirts of the town, among the neat residences of Haversack Street and Elmwood Avenue; and sat down for a moment on a low stone wall, to rest.

Farther out, at Eddie's Place, the red neon lights flashed, and the music played. Waiters hurried to and fro inside, and cars drove up from Rivertown, and from as far away as Yuleville and Des Plaines. But just the same, although it was only a little after ten o'clock, a group of four young people were already going home.

Penelope Andrews had had a bad evening. She had arranged to go out with Marvin Greene, in Marvin's little car, and she had naturally expected to spend the entire evening with him. But Marvin had stopped to pick up his friend Henry Klum, and Henry's girl, Gloriana Bast; and somehow or other, Gloriana had got to sit up in front with Marvin, while Penelope was left to sit behind in the rumble seat, with Henry Klum.

And at Eddie's Place, where they had gone to dance, it was the same thing over again: Marvin danced with Gloriana, and left Penelope to Henry. It was only too easy to see that Marvin and Gloriana already understood each other, and were without a care in the world.

So Penelope had asked to go home early, which satisfied Henry Klum, who was bored with Penelope, and uneasy about the way things were turning out.

Now she sat in one corner of the rumble seat, gazing with hot eyes at the back flap of the canvas top which separated her from Marvin and Gloriana. Mr. Klum, after an awkward and half-hearted attempt to hold her hand, had huddled down in his corner to doze; and Penelope brooded. The wind blew through her hair, the cold air chilled her face, and her entire chest felt sore and heavy with the pain in her heart.

This was the end, between herself and Marvin. It was cruel, that it should come on such a beautiful night, instead of during a storm, or in the middle of winter, with everything icy and frozen. But that was all that beauty was for, to add to people's pain; just like in the movies, where there was always music when people were dying. When she thought what it would be like to wake up in the morning and not be in love any more, she felt that she could not bear to live.

The small coupé rattled home toward Rivertown, its motor, without a muffler, popping like a string of firecrackers, while Marvin and Gloriana, hidden by the canvas top, sang comfortably together in the front seat. "I'm just a prisoner of love," they sang, which Penelope, fortunately, did not hear.

The coupé drew up at Penelope's house, on Elmwood Avenue; and Penelope climbed stiffly out of the rumble seat. There was no use asking anyone to come in. "Good night," she said sourly, to no one in particular; "thank you for the evening." And she added in what she hoped was an airy way:

"See you again some day."

Mr. Klum waved a vague hand, Mr. Greene smiled amiably, and Miss Bast gazed out at her with a puzzled look, as though she were a little uncertain as to just who Penelope was. Then the car rocketed off, leaving her standing alone, and wanting to cry.

She turned slowly toward the house. Well, that was that; that was the end of everything.

And she drew a long, quivering breath of fury and despair.

At that moment, someone gave a dry cough in the darkness, and turning with a start, she saw Mr. Whittle sitting in the shadows on the low stone wall, within a few feet of her.

In her sudden fright, she took a step toward him, to make sure. "What are you doing here?" she asked harshly. She did not mean to be rude, but she was startled; she felt that she had been spied on. Mr. Whittle made a small, apologetic gesture. "I didn't know it was your house," he said. "I was walking, and sat down to rest."

"Oh," said Penelope. She hesitated, not knowing what to say next. "Well . . ." she began.

She took another step toward him; she was afraid that she had made a bad impression. "I must have thought you were a robber, or something," she said; and smiled shyly, in what she meant to be a friendly way.

110

But suddenly she felt embarrassed, and did not know what to do.

"I guess I ought to be going in," she said uncertainly.

Mr. Whittle looked around him at the quiet street, with its shadowy lawns and houses on which the moonlight lay like a dream, peaceful and serene. And all at once he did not feel weary or unhappy any more; but he did not want her to go in and leave him.

"It's not very late," he said.

It was strange, she thought: she didn't really want to go in. Though she had never imagined that she would want to sit out in the moonlight with Mr. Whittle, either. But she was restless; and there was nothing to do inside. . . .

Nothing to do but think about Marvin Greene. . . .

She put her hand on the stone, to see how damp it was. She needn't actually sit there; she could just lean against it for a few minutes . . . it was, she had to admit, a dreamy night, with the moonlight making shadows over everything. . . .

With a young and graceful gesture, she lifted herself onto the wall beside him. "I guess I don't have to go right in," she said.

And she waited for him to say something interesting or illuminating.

Mr. Whittle said nothing; but he seemed to relax suddenly, as though something sharp had given way inside. He remained silent, smiling a little sadly to himself. She did not actually turn her head to look at him, but after a while, when he still did not say anything, she glanced at him sideways, from under her long, dark lashes. In the moonlight, his face looked worn and stern, no longer old, but refined by experience and grief. He looked like a stranger; he could be anyone at all, she thought, as long as she didn't keep telling herself that it was Professor Whittle. She wondered what he was thinking about.

"I guess you're glad the year is almost over," she said at last, to make conversation.

"Am I?" he answered. He seemed surprised, as though it were something he hadn't thought of before. "Are you?" he asked.

112

He answered himself before she could reply. "Yes, I suppose you are," he said. "Because, for you, tomorrow is just as lovely as today."

She leaned back on her hands, brooding, her chin on her chest. Tomorrow? What was lovely about tomorrow? "I wish it were a long time after tomorrow," she said.

He turned to look at her, in surprise. In the near-darkness, she seemed neither young nor old, but ageless, like the night, and sorrowful, and wise. "Why do you wish it were a long time after tomorrow?" he asked gently.

"Oh, I don't know," she said; "I just do."

She turned away from him, and then looked slowly back again, in a puzzled way. It was strange, sitting there beside him in the shadows. . . . It was strange because it didn't seem at all unnatural. It was almost as if they were friends, or something. "I don't know," she said again, vaguely.

A star splashed downward in the sky, above the trees; and she caught her breath. "Oh," she cried. "Look."

113

"Did you wish on it?" he asked, smiling. She shook her head. "I forgot," she said. "It went so fast."

"They say it's lucky when a star falls," he said. "I don't know why."

The stone under her was uneven, and after a moment she moved a shade closer to him. The mood of her bitterness had passed; she was still unhappy, but it was a different unhappiness, cold, and quick, and restless. It was queer, too, because they hadn't actually said very much; and yet it seemed to her that they had already said a great deal . . . though she couldn't think what. She had a feeling that he would understand her . . . if he was aware of her.

"Nothing is very lucky," she said; and it seemed to him that she shivered, as if she were cold.

He was almost achingly aware of her; he could feel her firm young shoulder pressing against him, ever so lightly. Warmth came from her body, and the faint fragrance of perfume.

"You're not very happy, are you?" he said gently.

114

"Who is?" she whispered.

No one is happy, he thought; and at the same time he was relieved to think that she was unhappy. And with a sudden, overwhelming feeling of tenderness toward her, he put out his hand, to draw the coat closer around her neck. "Are you sure you're warm enough?" he asked.

"Yes," she said, looking at him with her dark, wondering eyes. "Are you?"

They stared at each other for a long moment, without speaking. And in that moment, which seemed to have no end, they looked deep into each other's eyes, and saw there only themselves. Almost as if against her will, she swayed a little toward him; and a strand of her hair brushed across his face. Mr. Whittle's throat turned dry.

"It's getting late," he said.

"Is it?" she murmured. Her eyes appeared to be closed; she might almost have been dreaming. . . .

It seemed to Mr. Whittle that the night smelled of honeysuckle, although he knew that it was too early for honeysuckle. The night poured its sweetness over the earth, and over the two of them where they sat side by side in the hush of moonlight. . . . The night breathed with a mysterious sound all around them, and their hearts replied with mystery.

Oh lovely night, Oh lovely night.

"Lean back, against my arm," he said.

Penelope did not answer. She felt suddenly a little breathless, the way she did sometimes when something was about to happen. The night bent over her, it bent over Mr. Whittle too, as though it had taken them both into its arms. . . .

Mr. Whittle looked around at the sleeping houses. "I must go," he said.

She did not move, or look up. "Must you?" she murmured. "I don't know."

"Do you want me to stay?"

"I think so," she said.

Her hand, small, soft, and warm, and curled like a leaf, lay near his own. Without deciding anything, almost without volition, their fingers touched, and then clung together; and she dropped her head against his shoulder. "People will see us," she murmured.

"No," he said. And he thought: Why do we

think so much about what other people are doing in the world? They are not thinking about us . . . each one of us is alone in the world forever. Each in his own dark night. . . .

"We mustn't do this," she whispered.

And tomorrow? he thought; who knows when tomorrow will come? Or if it will come at all?

He reached out, and put his arm around her. "Only this moment is clear," he said; "only this night is beautiful."

He sat looking down at her, waiting, with a troubled smile on his face. As though she knew that he was looking at her, she slowly lifted her face, pale in the moonlight, ineffably young and tender; and smiled in a bewildered way. "What did you say?" she murmured; and lifted her mouth toward his.

What am I doing? thought Mr. Whittle with a groan.

A moment later a car went by, flooding the pavement with its headlights; but Mr. Whittle did not pay any attention to it.

Penelope did not notice it either. Her eyes were closed; her parted lips were raised for another kiss. After a moment she nodded gently. "Yes," she said. She did not know what had been asked of her, or what she was saying yes to; she only knew that somewhere in the night, in the silence, and the cold, sweet air, she had lost the heavy weight from her heart. A stranger held her in his arms; he was no one, he was love itself. She forgot the disasters of the day; she forgot tomorrow. . . .

"Oh you," she murmured. "You!"

CHAPTER

Ten

WHEN MR. WHITTLE left the house he left
Amanda weeping upstairs in her room. She was
weeping not so much for Mr. Whittle, but for
herself, because she was tired and angry, and
because she had not expressed herself very well.
After a while, the tears ceased, leaving her with
hiccups; and she came downstairs again, to prepare the evening meal for her family. But Mr.
Whittle was gone.

It was some time before Lucinda missed him;
and by then she was already half way through
her supper. "Where's father?" she asked, looking around the table with surprise; "isn't he
coming home?"

"I don't know," said Amanda honestly.

Lucinda's sharp eyes missed nothing. She
spread a piece of bread with peanut butter, and

crammed it into her mouth. "I like being alone like this," she said; "just the two of us."

Amanda smiled at her woefully. "Do you, dear?" she asked.

"Just us women," said Lucinda. She gave her mother a speculative look; the evening was full of possibilities, if she used them right. "Mother . . . " she began.

"Yes, Lucinda?"

"Was father as old as Marvin Greene when he was married?"

"Older," said Amanda. "Lots older."

"Marian can dance the rumba," said Lucinda. "Marvin taught her."

She leaned hopefully forward in her chair. "Can I go over there tonight after supper?" she asked.

"Not tonight," said Amanda. "I want you to stay here, with me."

"Well," said Lucinda, "can we go to the movies, then?"

"No, dear," said Amanda. "I have work to do."

Lucinda screwed her face up in despair. "Oh,

heck," she exclaimed; "I never have any fun."
And she added:

"I don't see the good of being married, if you
have to work all the time."

"You'll see the good of it some day," said
Amanda; "when you're old."

"I'm never going to be old," cried Lucinda.
"I'm going to die when I'm twenty-five.

"Besides," she wound up, "Father says we're
all going to blow up soon, anyhow."

Amanda thought to herself: even Lucinda re-
members that nonsense. But there are lots of
different ways of blowing up. And for the tenth
time she wished that she had kept her voice down
when she was arguing with Robert.

After Lucinda had helped her mother with
the dishes, had read the comics, telephoned to
Ellen, done her homework, and used up five
pieces of paper drawing a picture of Ralph
Wender, who came out looking like a teacup
with spots, she went to bed. Then Amanda took
her sewing into Mr. Whittle's study, and tried
to keep from worrying. It wasn't like Robert to
go off like that . . . or to stay away so long.

He must be very angry indeed, not even to come home for supper. Of course, she'd been right; he had no business to make a fool of himself in front of all those people, particularly when he had a wife and daughter to consider, and his daughter in school, and a member of the Girl Scouts. It certainly was discouraging, to try to make a place for yourself in the community, and then have it all turn into shards and pottles. Maybe that wasn't the name for it exactly, but it was something of the sort. . . .

Still, she supposed, she needn't have spoken to him quite so bitterly. She supposed, if she was fair, she'd have to admit that he had tried hard. It wasn't his fault that they were poor . . . though there were others poorer, as far as that was concerned. And after all, supposing they didn't have as much money as the Blaneys; was that so awful? Lots of people didn't, and belonged to the St. Vincent Club, and the Daughters of the American Revolution.

Lucinda was much too young to understand about marriage, even if she tried to explain it to her. There was a lot you couldn't explain, anyway, to a twelve-year-old; not possibly. And as for the rest — of course it was work, hard work; but it was worth it. She'd never wanted anything else in her life, just her own home, and the strength to keep it; and a little admiration now and then, to keep her spirits up. From her husband, of course . . . or somebody. . . .

Her parents had never thought much of Robert, but they were wrong; Robert worked hard, and he had a wonderful mind. He should have had something better than Amanda. Just the same, it was homes like theirs that made up the nation; maybe she'd never learned to do the rumba, but she could make biscuits, and iron a shirt, and that was more than her mother could do. Or half the members of the Literary and Historical Society. Or Lucinda, either, the way she was going.

You weren't young very long, she thought; and when it was over, it was over. She had no patience with people who tried to fool themselves that life was all hoop-la, and going to the movies . . . or driving around all night in their cars. . . .

123

There were a lot of accidents on the roads, too, these days. And suddenly her needle wavered, her hand shook, and she looked up from her sewing in alarm. Supposing something had happened to Robert, wandering around out there in the dark?

He had never stayed out so long before. Usually he just went around the block a few times, and then came home and refused to talk to anyone.

Immediately she saw him stretched out on the pavement, crushed, mangled, and already breathing his last. It was her own fault; she had driven him away.

Thoroughly alarmed by this time, she lifted the telephone off its cradle, to call the police station. However, at the last minute, she decided to call Mr. and Mrs. Blaney instead.

"Could I come over for a little while?" she asked; "that is, if you're not busy?" She would just run in, she thought, and come right home again; and perhaps when she got back, Robert would be there. The way a child would make believe it didn't care — and wasn't looking. . . .

124

The Blaneys were delighted to see her, and offered her ginger ale, and were a little surprised when she chose whisky instead. "I seem to be alone tonight," she said apologetically; "Robert is working. . . ."

And she looked around with a humble smile, as though to say What happiness, to have a husband who is a banker, and not a genius.

Mrs. Blaney clucked sympathetically. "You mustn't let Robert work too hard," she said, "with the hot weather coming."

"No indeed," said Mr. Blaney. His mouth drew in at the corners, the way it did at the bank, when he was studying an interesting bundle of securities. So you're alone, he thought; and felt himself brighten up, in a wary way.

"All work, and no play," he remarked. "Ha ha."

And he looked gloomily over at his wife, who was busy with her sewing.

"I always say to Alfred not to work too hard," remarked Mrs. Blaney. "Don't I, Alfred?"

"Oh, well," said Mr. Blaney comfortably. He was pleased to have people think that he worked too hard, and that without him things would be in a bad way. "We have to pay our little bills," he said, with a jovial wink at Amanda.

"It isn't the money that worries Robert," said Amanda. "It's the examinations."

"They'll be over soon," said Mrs. Blaney.

Amanda took a long drink from her glass. Nothing is over soon, she thought drearily; everything just goes on and on. How can you hope to tell people about yourself, ever? People are all alone. . . .

"I haven't been able to get any number fifty thread," remarked Mrs. Blaney, "since the middle of April. What I've got now won't hardly last me out the month."

"I just use anything," said Amanda, "so long as the color is right."

"Well, I don't know," said Mrs. Blaney. "I like to have things nice."

Her needle flashed for a moment in the lamplight. "I like them nice," she said, "even where they don't show."

Yes, thought Amanda; if you could only have things nice all over. But how did you go about it? that was the thing. You were always trying to get along without something you needed. . . .

"I never seem to have the time," she said.

"You can always find the time if you've a mind to," said Mrs. Blaney. "Still, what I always say is, each to his own way. Don't I, Alfred?"

"That's right," said Mr. Blaney, genially. "Each to his own way."

"That's what makes the world go round," said Amanda.

"Nobody sees things just the same," said Mr. Blancy.

Mrs. Blaney laid her sewing down in her lap, and made a totally unexpected remark. "Well, I don't know," she said gently. "When you've lived with somebody as long as I've lived with Alfred, you get to see things pretty much the same."

She sat looking in front of her with a peaceable expression. "And when you come to add it all up," she said, "it adds up just about as much one way as another."

She picked up her sewing again. "I don't know

but what that's one of the hardest things in the world to learn," she said.

Amanda lifted her nose out of her glass, and looked around her at the comfortable room. It was so quiet and pleasant at the Blaney's; they got along so well, they never seemed to argue about anything. There was something really good, she thought, about Ruth Blaney. . . . And all at once she realized that she felt a lot more cheerful. When she tried to remember what she and Robert had quarreled about, it all seemed very hazy, and far away in her mind. Maybe they hadn't really quarreled at all. And in a sudden hurry to return to her house, and to Robert, she finished her drink, and exclaimed:

"I mustn't keep you any longer."

Mr. Blaney had been watching Amanda with bright and tender interest. But he was careful not to show any of it on his face. He tried to imagine what she looked like under her blouse — her round, white shoulders, and the hollow between her neck and her collar bone. He did not let himself go any further, for reasons of deli-

cacy, and because he did not want to excite
himself.

"I'll take you home," he said. "The walk will
do me good."

It was cooler out of doors, the air was fresh
and sweet, and Amanda found that she was in
less of a hurry than she had thought. It was
pleasant to be walking along the street, with the
leaves making a dapple of moonlight around
her, and Mr. Blaney being attentive at her side.
Once or twice, he took her arm to help her over
a rough place in the sidewalk; she didn't need
it, but she rather liked it, it made her feel delicate.

"Ruth is such a dear," she said. "She's such a
lovely person, really."

Mr. Blaney agreed with her. "She's a good
woman," he said; "the backbone of the country."
At the same time, he could not keep himself from
thinking about other parts of the body.

"You've been very happy together, haven't
you?" said Amanda wistfully. "All these years."

"We have, indeed," said Mr. Blaney. And he
added, in a brave way:

"Ruth is a splendid woman."

"That's what I mean," said Amanda; but she was not entirely sure that she knew just what she meant. It seemed to take a little more energy to speak than she was used to, and her legs felt heavy; perhaps she ought not to have finished her drink so fast, but she felt very comfortable, and even happy. . . .

"It was nice of you to come in tonight," said Mr. Blaney. "You must do it more often."

"It was just an idea," said Amanda. And she added, almost with surprise, as though she had just thought of it:

"I was all alone."

Mr. Blaney gave a deep sigh, and gently squeezed her arm. "You oughtn't to be alone," he said. "I wouldn't leave you alone if you belonged to me."

For some reason this amused Amanda, and she gave a little laugh, not unlike a giggle. "I'm sorry," she said; "I belong to Robert."

"I know," said Mr. Blaney heavily. And he added solemnly:

"Does he appreciate what he has?"

"I guess so," said Amanda uncertainly. "What has he?" she asked a moment later.

"You," said Mr. Blaney tenderly.

"I guess he does," said Amanda. "I don't know."

She found that she was walking more slowly, and that Mr. Blaney had taken her arm, and had forgotten to let it go. It didn't matter; she was in no hurry to get anywhere. If Robert was home, he would simply have to wait for her; she'd had to wait for him. After all, he was the one who had gone slamming out of the house. . . .

She gave a deep, quivering sigh. "Oh well," she said.

"What's the matter?" asked Mr. Blaney.

"Nothing," she answered. "It's only that — things get mixed up sometimes."

"They certainly do," replied Mr. Blaney. His hand seemed to tremble a little on her arm. "Things certainly get mixed up," he said.

"Robert and I are very fond of each other," said Amanda. "I wouldn't ever want to do anything to hurt him." And she peered up, in a friendly, puzzled way, into Mr. Blaney's face.

"Would I?" she asked.

They were approaching Amanda's house; and their steps grew slower and slower. "I wouldn't ever want to do anything," she said, "like — like . . .

". . . to make him unhappy," she wound up.

"No indeed," said Mr. Blaney hoarsely.

She looked at Mr. Blaney, she saw his sober, conscientious face, worked on by some secret emotion; she saw, in her mind, the peaceful and comfortable Blaney home, all in its aura of dignity and repose, and his quiet and respectable wife, with her successful history behind her. *If you add it all up in the end,* she thought, *it adds up to just as much one way as another.* The only thing was — did it? And bowing her head, suddenly, unaccountably, she wept. "Here, here," said Mr. Blaney in astonishment; "what's this?"

"I don't know," she whispered.

Half frightened at his own daring, and with an uncertain gesture, he put his arm around her, and patted her shoulder. "What's the matter?" he asked; his throat felt dry, and his voice trembled.

She shook her head. "Nothing," she said.

She could not have told him, she could not have put it into words. It was so many things . . . like not being young any more, and knowing that the past was over and would never come again. It was not knowing what had happened to all the bright years. . . . It was being afraid of the future, which lay so dry and pinched ahead of her; it was thinking how she had quarreled with Robert, it was thinking that nobody loved her . . . it was being ashamed. . . .

Because she knew in her heart that none of it was true. The bright years had come and gone for her like everybody else; the future was what she would make it. Love was for her to give. . . . And whose fault was it that she and Robert had quarreled?

"Hold me a little," she whispered.

They stood in the light of a street lamp in front of her house, her head against his chest, his arms awkwardly around her. He could not think of anything to say; now that it had happened, he was bewildered, lost in blissful anxiety. One of his legs started to go to sleep, and he shifted his weight to the other one. "My dear," he murmured; "my dear."

She looked up at him after a while, with wet eyes, and a woeful smile. "I'm sorry," she said. And reaching up, she took his face in her hands, and drew it down to her.

"You're sweet," she said, and kissed him.

It was at this moment that Mr. Whittle, walking slowly home as though in a dream, his mind one moment a complete blank, the next filled with ineffable delight, with remorse, and with the blackest forebodings, turned the corner and saw them.

C H A P T E R

Eleven

THE SHOCK was tremendous.

Mr. Whittle did not see Amanda run quickly into the house; he did not wait to see Mr. Blaney, after standing a moment in reverent silence, start briskly but soberly home again. Instead, he turned, and headed back toward the River Road, in a daze.

He could not understand what had happened to him. One moment he had been an ordinary man, happy, frightened, full of doubts and excuses, but with his own decisions to make, and in command of the situation; and the next moment he had lost everything, was homeless, bewildered, and had been betrayed by his wife and the vice president of a bank.

Mr. Whittle would not have believed it was possible to suffer such anguish; but at the same time the shock seemed to have numbed his senses, and this kept him from a full realization of his feelings. His most immediate emotion was one of intense loneliness; like a child whose mother has suddenly disappeared in a crowded department store, he felt lost, abandoned, and a prey to the most dreadful accidents. How was it going to be possible for him to live? The future closed in upon him like a wall — a future without security, without a family, even without anyone to make him breakfast in the morning, or to take his temperature when he was sick. It seemed to him that he was unable to breathe; and although he felt cold as ice, he found that he had broken out into a sweat. He thought of all the things that Amanda did for him, day after day — the small, endless, confusing, difficult duties and favors. . . . Now he would have to do them all for himself.

For he understood that there was nothing for them to do but leave each other. It was not from any guilt on his part, for he no longer felt guilty of anything: the guilt was Amanda's. He did not blame her, but that did not lessen the anguish he felt, or the sudden sense of being lost in the world. I have been a failure, he said to himself: while I immersed myself in the past, my wife was taken away from me by somebody else; while I dreamed of the great empires of the world, I lost my own.

He could not understand why she had chosen Alfred Blaney, who was older than he, and not attractive in a physical way. But then he remembered that Mr. Blaney was a wealthy man, and this shocked him, at the same time that it comforted him in an obscure way. It is the fault of the economic system, he thought, rather than a personal lack on my part.

Now that he had lost her, she seemed infinitely attractive and desirable to him. He remembered her myriad kindnesses, and her little ways, many of which had irritated him, but which he now believed used to enchant him. There was never anyone like her, he thought; she was such a good housekeeper, nothing was too much trouble for her. But that would all go to someone else, now; someone else would get the benefit of it. She was no longer his; she belonged to the world, or she belonged to herself. . . .

And he imagined her free and happy, smiling in a gracious way, and enjoying herself with Mr. Blaney, or with some even more attractive people, and not thinking about him at all. Look, he wanted to cry out to her, I am frightened . . . I am very unhappy. Do not leave me like this. . . .

It was too late: she had already left him.

He bowed his head upon his breast; now I am really alone, he thought. Of course, there was Penelope, but he was not yet ready to think of Penelope, that would come later. She did not seem as attractive now; she was scarcely more than a child. In any case, he had never meant to leave Amanda, or to be unfaithful to her in a serious way.

And besides, no one had seen him.

But he had seen Amanda and Alfred Blaney. And at the thought of this woman, whom he knew so well, whose voice, scent, flesh, hair, and underclothes were so familiar to him, melting with expectation in another man's arms, he felt

a sudden wave of sickness and despair; and re-
membering how he had seen her put her arms up
to Mr. Blaney with such a tender gesture, he
gave a loud groan. I would rather be dead, he
exclaimed, than have to imagine what has been
going on here.

But then, like a thunderclap, it occurred to
him that he would soon be dead in any case, and
Amanda and Mr. Blaney also. It should have
come as more of a consolation to him than it did.

For he was quite certain that he wanted death
for himself and for the world: to become nothing, to cease to exist, to be no more than a nebu-
lous gas, floating among the stars, in infinite
space, without memory or identity, without a
name or a future, without habits, without grief
or shame. . . .

And once again, as earlier, he looked up at
the clear, dew-frosty night, at the wind-bitten
sky in which the moon was almost down behind
a bank of black clouds. Let all this end, he said,
in one swift and merciful moment; and let mankind be absolved of its destiny, which has been
to suffer, and destroy.

At the same time, he could not repress a feeling of despair, at the golden opportunities which had been thrown away.

For he realized that he, too, had wasted something that had been precious to him; and that there was something to be said for the monastic life after all, and the serene happiness of those who denied the world and the flesh.

The moon sank below the silver rim of the dark cloud-bank, and the air turned colder. A hush enveloped the earth; the wind died down, the stars became obscured, and lightning flashed in the distance. Mr. Whittle sat among the damp ferns above the river, whose sound he could hear below him, and smelled the river-smell, of rotted wood and fungus, of birch, moss, and water.

How many worlds are around me, he thought, unseen and undreamt of in the void — of which this one of ours is the smallest and the least conspicuous. Yet on this earth we have an animal called man, which is to say that he has a spine but no tail, two arms, hands with five fingers each, one of them the invaluable thumb; and so

140

on. He was made, we are told, in the image of God; so it is not surprising that we worship a Being who also has thumbs, and no tail, two eyes, a beard, and so on. But supposing that on some planet of a small star, in one tiny cluster among the infinite clusters of the Milky Way, there are beings with the heads of cockroaches, and the bodies of mermaids — what then?

"Well," he said, looking up at the sky, "how do You answer that?"

Immediately an image of God began to form in the air above his head, in the direction of the approaching storm. Looking a little like Dr. Thirkel, God gazed down at him from the bank of clouds, with a serious expression.

"I have many forms," said God: "I have been fire, air, running streams, the sun, meat, wine, silence, and the noonday shade. Do you imagine that I would be satisfied to look like you and Mr. Blaney?"

"Perhaps not," said Mr. Whittle humbly, "because we are not very good examples. But there are others among us."

And he added loyally:

"Amanda, at least, is beautiful."

"Not to a bark beetle," said God. "Beauty is in the eye of the beholder; and so am I."

"Still," said Mr. Whittle stubbornly, "there is great beauty in mankind; and if You are going to destroy us, I wish that You would leave some memory of us somewhere in the universe."

"You worry too much about what is going to happen," said God. "Who told you that I was going to destroy anything?"

"Already," said Mr. Whittle simply, "the fourth angel has poured his bowl upon the sun. 'And it was given unto it to scorch men with fire.'"

"Ah," said God, with satisfaction; "you have been reading John. What do you make of it? Much of it is purely local, of course."

"One must consider the times in which it was written, I suppose," said Mr. Whittle.

"The times are a lot worse now," said God.

He was silent for a moment, and then continued moodily:

142

"Sometimes I think it was a mistake for Me to have created man, or at least to have made him so irresponsible. 'And the rest of mankind, who were not killed with these plagues, repented not of the work of their hands, nor of their murders, nor of their fornication, nor of their thefts.' "

"I have never stolen anything," said Mr. Whittle.

"You never murdered anybody, either," replied God severely; "but I mentioned all three."

The wind had risen; a sudden puff sighed in the ferns, and in the reeds of the river. The lightning flashed closer; and thunder reverberated among the hills near at hand. "Very well," said Mr. Whittle, bowing his head in resignation: "destroy us then; but get on with it, please."

"A moment ago," said God, "you asked Me to leave some memory of you here on earth. Now you are in a hurry to be annihilated. Make up your mind.

"The truth is," He continued wistfully, "I do

not want to destroy you at all. I am more anxious than you for the fate of mankind, and I would like to save as much of it as possible. I am fond of this earth, with its fields and green meadows, its wind-dark seas, its tall trees and exquisite flowers. Even the birds delight Me, despite their angry quarrels. But it is only in man that I can enjoy these sights and sounds, that I have, as it were, a seat at the festival. I look out at My handiwork through his eyes; and it is through his nose that I smell the aroma of summer. He is My protagonist on earth, a mortal witness to My existence; without him I should see only what a spider sees, hear only the clicking language of the lobster and crab, or the endless whispering of the leaves. It will be a long while before a spider writes a symphony, or a mouse builds a cathedral.

"It was My hope that man would never learn the secret of his own destruction; and it was for this reason that I forbade Adam to eat of the fruit of the tree of knowledge. I knew that knowledge would do him no good; but he knew better."

And He gave a deep sigh.

"If it has to be," said Mr. Whittle, "it has to be. It is the waiting around that I don't like; why not get it over with?"

"Don't rush Me," said God; "I am trying to think of a way out."

"There is no way out," said Mr. Whittle. "Amanda has left me."

A sudden sough of wind swept down on him from across the river, a blinding flash of lightning lit the sky, and with a deafening crack of thunder, the storm broke upon him. Mr. Whittle turned his face up to the rain; he bared his soul to the lightning, which flashed in a terrifying way up and down the river-valley. "It is not my fault," he exclaimed, "that I was born to love beauty, to grow old, and to die. I am not to blame for the longings of my heart and the hunger of my mind, for the thirst for delight and the desire for happiness. Nor am I to be held to account for the pain I have been obliged to give others, or have received myself; for it could all have been arranged differently, and with less confusion. I am innocent; and my destruction is unwarranted, and irrelevant."

There was a final ear-shattering crash in the air, and God spoke; as usual, He had the last word.

"Nonsense," He said.

Twelve

THE WORLD did not end that night; the storm roared on to the east, banging its kettledrums above Yuleville and Prairie Falls; and in the morning the sun rose again over Rivertown, and sparkled on the wet sidewalks, and on the fresh, green leaves, dark with the night's drenching.

In Penelope's room, the dotted swiss curtains stirred gently in the cool, morning air; robins sang on the lawn outside her window, and a yellow finger of light touched her sleeping cheek, warm and rosy on the pillow. She sighed, and smiled; and opening her eyes, lay for a moment staring at the ceiling.

She was confused, and did not know, for a moment, whether to be happy or sad. And like someone awakening from an accident or an operation, she cautiously explored her feelings; she put out gentle inquiries, and waited to see how she felt.

But she could not feel anything, except her own healthy body, a morning drowsiness, and an appetite for breakfast.

Yawning, she rose, and went to the window to let the sun shine on her face still flushed with sleep. She breathed the air washed by the rain, she smelled the warm, summer-smell of wet grass and drenched earth; and at that very moment she felt the first shiver of excitement at the thought of seeing Mr. Whittle again.

The night came back to her; out of the comfortable haze of sleep, it appeared suddenly in her memory. How strange . . . nothing could have been more unexpected, or unlikely. And yet it was true, it had happened. With Professor Whittle . . . of all people.

And with a surprised smile, she thought how she would come into the classroom, and see him sitting behind his desk, just as usual. . . . Only it wouldn't be just as usual. Not any more; not after what had happened. Because now, when they looked at each other, there would always be that secret between them. . . .

She was barely eighteen, and she had been kissed by a grown-up man. She remembered how stern and rueful he had looked, not at all like a college boy, but more like a leader of men; and yet, when he had kissed her, it had felt just like Marvin Greene, or even more exciting.

At the thought of Marvin Greene, she gave a pout of disdain, to balance the sudden feeling of loss she experienced, somewhere near her heart, or a little lower.

Leaning on the bureau, she gazed earnestly and for a long while at her reflection in the mirror. Did Mr. Whittle really think that she was beautiful? She smiled a little in the glass; she gave herself up to shy dreams, they floated through her mind like summer clouds.

After a while she caught her lower lip between her teeth. "Penelope Andrews!" she whispered to herself in amazement. For it seemed to her that she had been chosen to play a lovely part in the world. How strange life was; and how happy one could be, after all . . . to wake at eighteen on a bright May morning. . . .

At breakfast she maintained a starry attitude, and ate her cereal with an air of abstraction. She felt herself already anointed; but she did not know whether she should stay to speak to Mr. Whittle after class or not.

"Your teacher gave us such an interesting talk the other day," said her mother. "All about the end of the world. Or at least I think that was what it was about; there was something about some people who lived ten thousand years ago, and ate camels, which strikes me as rather horrid; I shouldn't at all like to eat a camel, but then I don't care for pig's feet either, and your father adores them."

Penelope looked at her blankly. In her mind's eye, she saw herself walking with Professor Whittle across the campus, while everybody turned to look at them with expressions of surprise. At the same time, people could not help admiring her, for her air of poise, and her smiling and gracious expression. She is a strange, unusual girl, they said; no one expected anything like this.

"I wish you wouldn't put so much butter on your toast," said Mrs. Andrews unhappily, "if you don't mean to eat it. We have only half a pound left, and it's almost impossible to get."

From far away, as though in a dream, Penelope heard her mother's voice discussing the market situation, and the storm of the night before. She did not answer; there was no need to. The world was full of beauty; summer was coming in, and loveliness was all around. What was it he had said? "Only this moment is clear . . ." and then he had kissed her. Soon the honeysuckle would be in blossom, and after that, roses; moonlight came often, and the dark was sweet. Summer was full of golden light and green shadows, of whispers and drowsy voices; summer was full of lovely fragrance. . . . And so was her heart.

She wanted it to be like that always . . . even in autumn, when the maples were yellow on the hills, and the wood-smoke hung blue and hazy in the air. . . .

Only this moment is clear. But a moment could go on and on, forever.

She walked to class, through the bright, sunny morning; and the moment kept going on, in her heart and all around her. It was like a rill of clear water; she had never noticed how green the leaves were, or how many climbing roses there were over the campus walls; she had never been so uplifted, and attentive. She wondered where Mr. Whittle was, and what he was doing; she wondered if he was thinking about her, too.

She wondered what he would look like, and what he would say; she imagined how she would sit in her seat, and glance up at him from under her lashes. But now, if their eyes met, he would not look away. . . . She thought that she was happy because she was thinking about him. I suppose I am in love with him, she thought.

She did not know that she was in love with love, and with Penelope Andrews; and that she would never be in love with anyone else, her whole life long.

I am in love with Professor Whittle, she thought. And with a quickening heart, but in

152

a modest manner, she turned down toward the Arts and Sciences building.

"Penelope," someone said.

She did not expect to see him step out from behind a tree, unshaven, haggard, with wet and wrinkled clothes, and bloodshot eyes. "Penelope," he said hoarsely.

She stood stock-still, and stared at him, with her mouth open. Was this the man she had been dreaming about? And in a confused way, and with a frightened smile, she murmured:

"Good morning."

"I have to talk to you," said Mr. Whittle. He seemed to have a cold; his nose was slightly red, as though he had been blowing it. "Listen," he said.

But now that she was there, standing in front of him, he no longer knew exactly what he wanted to say. He had been waiting to see her . . . to be forgiven, perhaps, or to be comforted. Was that all he had wanted? Merely to see her again, before he went away? For there was no doubt in his mind that he was going to leave Rivertown and Caraway College. Or did he imagine that perhaps — by some miracle — if he were to ask her . . . ? Or that in a gentle and lovely way she would tell him not to go, but to stay, for her sake? He didn't know; he hadn't thought it out. All he knew was that he had to see her again.

And there she was, in the clear sunshine, in her young beauty; but it was not the same any longer.

It was not the same for Penelope, either; in fact, it was a profound shock to her. She stood there, trying to be polite, and looking anxiously over her shoulder from time to time, to see if anyone was coming. She could not believe that this was really Mr. Whittle — this man who was old enough to be her father, this strange-looking man in his wrinkled, untidy suit. Had she really lain for a moment in his arms? She couldn't believe it; it wasn't true. What could she have been thinking of? How could she? oh, how could she?

And blushing with shame, she murmured unhappily:

"Please don't let's talk about it."

Mr. Whittle looked at her for a long while without speaking, and in a pleading way; then he looked dazedly out over the campus. He understood as clearly as though she had said it that she thought him ridiculous and repulsive; and it was so different from what he had expected that it made him feel dizzy.

"I thought," he said slowly; "I guess I thought . . ."

Oh heavens, she cried to herself, let me get out of here. What if somebody should come along, and hear him? "You had no right," she said. "You had no right at all."

With all the strength of her heart, she wished that it was yesterday again; that she had never seen Mr. Whittle, that all this had never happened. She wanted to run away, to hide, to forget, to be washed free and clean. . . . She wanted her mother, her room with the dotted swiss curtains, the friends of her own age . . . she wanted Marvin Greene. Her eyes filled with tears of anger and self-pity.

"Go away," she whispered. "Please, please go away."

And turning suddenly, she fled down the path, hardly looking where she was going.

CHAPTER

Thirteen

AT LEAST one other person in Rivertown awoke
that morning in a state of confusion: and that
was Amanda. She had waited up till past mid-
night, watching the storm, and worrying, hop-
ing against hope that Mr. Whittle wasn't out
in it, and blaming herself for everything that
had happened; and she had fallen asleep at last
almost against her will, still listening for his step
at the door. When she awoke, the sun was shin-
ing, and for one blissful, sleepy moment she forgot her fears and her troubles; until she turned
over, and there was his bed, unused and un-
slept-in beside her, and her heart fell down like
a bird shot out of the sky.

I must keep my anxiety from Lucinda, she
thought. And in a quiet way, but with a pale

156

face, she went about getting breakfast as though
nothing had happened.

Lucinda did not ask any questions; she ac-
cepted with only mild surprise the obvious fact
that her father had not come home the night
before. Her first thought was that now she would
be able to see what trouble Dick Tracy had got
himself into, without having to look at the paper
upside down. As for what her parents did, or did
not do, it was of no concern to her one way or
another. Grown-ups led a meaningless life.

"Maybe father has been run over," she said;
and departed for school, without giving it any
further thought.

Left to herself, Amanda turned in a listless
way to her housework. But her mind wasn't on
it; she found herself staring at things for minutes at a time without seeing them, and giving
deep sighs. And all the while, her hands were
cold, her mind was as jumpy as a mouse, and
her ears were alert for the slightest sound from
outside. But there were only the usual morning
sounds, the calls of children, the barking of dogs,
the occasional passage of a car or a truck. The

street drowsed in the early sunshine, the peaceful, morning light washed the leaves outside the
window and lay in bars of green and yellow
across the floor; the house was full of the sound
of silence and the beating of Amanda's heart.
What was she to do?

She tried to think, to reason things out. Perhaps he had stayed the night somewhere; but
where? There were several small hotels. . . . Or
there could have been an accident. But then
oughtn't she to call the police? Still, if they had
found him, they would have notified her. And
in any case, the police . . . that was the last
resort; it made everything seem so hopeless.

And yet she couldn't simply sit there, waiting. . . .

And once again, not knowing what else to do,
she called the Blaneys. "Alfred," she said, "Robert hasn't come home yet."

Mr. Blaney was taken by surprise, for he had
forgotten all about Mr. Whittle. "Where is he?"
he asked.

"I don't know," said Amanda. "I think he has
left me."

And she waited for Mr. Blaney to tell her that such a thing was impossible.

Mr. Blaney put the phone back on its cradle with a thoughtful air. He was profoundly shocked, to say the least; and all the more so because he had not been expecting it. This is trouble, he thought: this is trouble indeed, and I want to have nothing to do with it. Nevertheless, he could not escape a slight feeling of guilt, which disturbed him; after all, he had made certain statements the night before, which he did not altogether remember, but which could easily have been misunderstood; he had even allowed himself — or almost allowed himself — or had he? — to be carried away, in a manner of speaking, which was certainly cause for alarm, things being the way they were. Amanda was a good-looking woman, she was an attractive woman; but she mustn't expect him to look after her, or anything like that; he was only a friend, after all, he had his own wife and home, thank you. . . .

No indeed; that little walk in the moonlight was much better forgotten. It had been a stupid thing to do, anyhow; suppose someone had seen him? He would be very sorry indeed if anything happened to Mr. Whittle; but why turn to him with it? Could she have thought . . . could she have imagined that he . . . did she suppose for a single moment that he meant to . . . ?

What a frightening thought! And with a severe and resolute frown, he hurried down to the bank, and left word with his secretary that if Mrs. Whittle called, he was, quite simply, out.

But Amanda did not want to talk to Mr. Blaney any more. Instead, she went to see Euphemia Warren, at the college. She did not know Euphemia very well, but she knew that Mr. Whittle knew her, and sometimes he stopped in at her studio for a cup of tea, after his classes. Perhaps Euphemia might have heard something; it was only a straw to catch at, but it was better than sitting at home alone, doing nothing — or calling the police. She was so worried and beside herself. . . .

When Euphemia Warren heard that Mr. Whittle had been missing all night, she lifted her eyebrows, and assumed a grave manner.

"Then it's true," she said; and added: "I must tell you: last night, as I drove home, I thought I saw him, but I was unable to correlate what I saw with what I thought I knew. That is so often the case, is it not? Otherwise, we should all be above ourselves."

"Yes?" asked Amanda impatiently. "Where was he?"

"On Elmwood Avenue," said Miss Warren, after a slight hesitation.

"Oh," said Amanda, disappointed. Elmwood Avenue covered a lot of territory. "He was walking," she said, taking it for granted.

"He was sitting down," said Miss Warren coldly.

It seemed to Amanda that the art instructress was keeping something back. "Did he look as though anything were the matter?" she asked.

Miss Warren again hesitated, and looked thoughtful and unhappy. "No," she said finally; "there didn't seem to be anything the matter."

"Well," said Amanda uncertainly, "perhaps if you could tell me where you saw him . . ."

"I don't know the number of the house," said

161

Miss Warren, "but I could take you there. If you think it would do any good," she added.

She felt sorry for Amanda; she wished she had not said anything at all. But perhaps it was all for the best. One could not always hope to correlate everything correctly.

"It's all I can think of to do," said Amanda. "If you don't mind."

Miss Warren took her to the house with the low stone wall, and waited while Amanda got out and looked anxiously around. But there was nothing unusual to be seen. "You're sure this is the place?" she asked.

Miss Warren nodded. "Yes," she said; "he was sitting right there. I had my lights on him."

It seemed absurd to go up to a strange house, and ring the bell, and ask if anyone had noticed a man sitting on the wall the night before. But what else was there to do? Supposing someone in the house *had* seen him, or spoken to him? Wasn't it worth looking like a fool, for the half minute it would take? Nevertheless, she hesitated before she rang the bell.

When the door opened, she was standing with

162

her back to it, looking at the low stone wall, and at Miss Warren's car beyond it. She turned quickly; and then for a moment she did not move at all.

Penelope Andrews stood in the doorway, looking at her with a sullen expression. She had been crying, her eyes were red, and her cheeks were pale. She did not recognize Amanda at first. "Mother isn't home," she said dully.

But then, all at once, she remembered having seen Amanda one night at the movies with Mr. Whittle. Of course; this was Mrs. Whittle. "Oh," she gasped; her eyes filled with fear, and putting her hand to her mouth, she turned in a panic, and fled into the house.

Amanda followed slowly. So, she thought; so. This is what Euphemia wouldn't tell me. It's been going on all the time, and I didn't know it.

Penelope had run into the library; she faced Amanda from the window corner, like a mouse at bay; she held her little paws out in front of her, as though to protect herself. "What do you want?" she cried. "I didn't do anything."

Amanda stood and looked at her. And in this

pretty, helpless, stupid child, dabbled with tears, and half frightened to death, she thought she saw the whole unhappy story of Mr. Whittle's strange behavior.

So that's what it was.

Penelope had sunk down on the window seat, and covered her face with her hands. "It wasn't my fault," she whispered; "really it wasn't."

"It wasn't anything."

"I'm sure it wasn't," said Amanda. "I'm sure it wasn't anything at all."

"I wish I were dead," said Penelope hopelessly.

"I'm afraid that wouldn't help," said Amanda.

She found herself trembling, and had to hold on to a chair for a moment. "Where is he?" she asked. "That's all I want to know."

"I don't know," wailed Penelope. "I don't know where he is. I never want to see him again."

And she burst into tears.

Amanda stood and looked at her; and her heart was full of anger and scorn. But at the same time she was afraid of what would happen to Mr. Whittle as a result of all this. You young people, she thought, you think you're very brave

164

and daring. You think you're hard and bright, you think that you can take care of yourselves, and never give anything back. You think that nothing will ever happen to you. Well, why shouldn't it? It happened to the dinosaurs. . . .

Oh God, she thought, I sound just like Robert.

She was not going to get any help from Penelope; she could see that. And so she turned to go. But before she went, she gave the weeping girl one last, stern look, full of moral indignation. "Whatever else you say," she remarked, "don't go blaming it on my husband. He's a bigger fool than I thought, but he doesn't go around making people do what they don't want to do.

"Maybe some day you'll have sense enough to know what you've done. I hope so. But meanwhile I wouldn't tell anybody about this, if I were you. I wouldn't tell anybody else at all."

C H A P T E R

Fourteen

Amanda returned to the car with a face like stone. "It was the wrong place after all," she said steadily. "No one was there all evening."

Miss Warren was not fooled; but she felt very sorry for her. "I might have been mistaken," she said. "It was really quite dark."

In this way they assured each other that they each knew everything there was to know. Miss Warren drove Amanda home, and left her; and Amanda went indoors with a strained smile, and a jaunty air. But the moment the door closed behind her, she tore upstairs as though the devil were after her, and flung herself upon the bed.

There, dry-eyed, she stormed by herself. For, despite what she had said to Penelope Andrews, she was more angry than anything else. Where Mr. Whittle might be — skyrocketing around, as she scornfully put it — seemed of less importance to her than the fact that she had been so outrageously betrayed. Betrayed? Worse than that: made a thorough fool of. What an utterly contemptible thing for him to have done. He didn't even have the decency to pick out a woman of his own age, like Euphemia Warren, or Mrs. Blaney; he had to pick out a child hardly older than Lucinda. A creature like a doll, without a thought in her head, and young enough to be his daughter.

His daughter: what would happen to her now, poor child? What would happen to the two of them? She could always take Lucinda home to her parents, she supposed, while she saw about getting a divorce. Lucinda wouldn't like it, and her parents would give her no peace, but that was the way life was, and that was what happened when people finally came out and showed their true natures. She would simply pack up, and get out, before he came back.

"I don't care if he never comes back," she said fiercely. "I hope I never see him again."

And thinking that she sounded too much like

167

Penelope Andrews, she raged afresh, at this new evidence of Mr. Whittle's villainy.

But in the midst of kicking with her feet on the counterpane, she suddenly stopped, raised her head, and listened. Someone was in the bathroom; she could hear the water running. Was it Lucinda, home from school? It was much too early for Lucinda, but on the other hand, this wasn't the day for the laundress. Puzzled, she lifted herself on her elbows. "Who's there?" she called.

There was no answer; whoever it was seemed to be gargling. Her eyes widened, she turned pale, clenched her fists, and cried out in a sharp voice: "Who is it?

"Is it you, Robert?"

She was answered by a sneeze; and a moment later Mr. Whittle appeared in the doorway, holding a glass of listerine in his hand. "I've caught a bad cold," he said.

Amanda had never wanted to see him again. But she had imagined him hard and defiant, or sheepish and ashamed of himself; and in any case an enemy, to be annihilated with a word, or with silence. Seeing him, on the contrary, pale and at the same time feverish, his hair untidy, his clothes wrinkled, his eyes and nose red and watery, she sprang up in alarm, and hurrying across the room, put her hand on his forehead. "You're sick," she said; "you've got a fever."

And taking the glass out of his hand, she herded him briskly back in the direction of his bed. "Get undressed," she said, "while I fix you something hot."

Numbly, Mr. Whittle allowed himself to be put to bed, and fed hot lemonade and aspirin. He was too tired and sick to object; and he no longer remembered very much of anything that had happened, or how he had seen Amanda in Mr. Blaney's arms. As the hours passed, his fever went higher; and in the late afternoon Amanda sent for the doctor, who left some sulfa tablets for him, and advised her to keep him as quiet as possible. "Let me know if anything happens," he said. "I'll come by again in the morning."

But in the morning there was no question about it: Mr. Whittle had pneumonia.

It was hard to breathe, and that frightened him. He lay in his bed, and stared at the ceiling, and took long, slow, painful breaths. It was strange when the ordinary, simple things that he was used to, like air, suddenly weren't there any more; when life itself was something that he had to keep reaching for, over and over again . . . with all his strength. . . .

It did not occur to him not to reach for it, or to let go; but it was tiring, and alarming. This wasn't what he was supposed to do in the world — all this should have been done for him. These lungs, which hurt so, which expanded and contracted so painfully and unwillingly — this heart which beat so heavily . . . they were not he, they were not Mr. Whittle. Mr. Whittle was something else: he was part of God's dream of the universe, he was the eyes through which God looked at the world. . . .

Amanda sat by the bedside, watching him, listening to the loud, slow breathing; and trying not to think of what it meant. But the truth was, for the first time that she could remember, she was terribly afraid. To her, too, this was not

Mr. Whittle; this laboring, struggling creature on the bed was not anyone she knew, but some tragic stranger, whose tenuous hold on life depended in some way upon herself. And in the very next moment she could see that it was indeed Mr. Whittle who was in pain, and frightened, and looked at her with pleading eyes. Oh God, she thought, don't let him die. Tell me what to do.

With a sick feeling, she thought of all the times she had been angry at him, for something he had done, or forgotten. She had usually been right; but what had been the good of it? She had thrown happiness away, time after time, for the sake of being right . . . and now she knew that she had only been right to love without thinking.

When I was young, she thought sadly, I did not live by the mind, but by the heart.

Give him back to me, God. I can forgive him for everything, except death.

Mr. Whittle was far away; his cloudy mind, ravaged by fever and deadened by drugs, imagined itself in a vast and airy place. It seemed to him that he was on the River Road again, while the darkness enveloped him, and the cold wind blew. And in the darkness, he heard God's voice; but he did not see Him.

"Well," said God quietly; "what did I tell you?"

Mr. Whittle bowed his head in resignation.

"Is it really time?" he asked humbly.

"What is time?" replied God. "Do you measure it by sequence, or by duration? You have already lived a lifetime in these last three days. Be satisfied with that."

Mr. Whittle cried out against the Invisible. "I am not satisfied," he cried; "I am not reconciled."

"That is the whole trouble with you," said God; and breathed a vast sigh in the darkness. "You are never satisfied."

He continued gently: "You have never understood anything despite your studies, and your M.A. degree. You have never known what was yours, what belonged to you and what did not. This is not My world because it is a pretty place to walk in, or because somebody has given it to

172

Me. It is Mine because it is the work of My hands; and for what I have put into it. If you have anything of your own, it is yours for the same reason."

"I had a home," said Mr. Whittle; "and a family."

"You were not satisfied with that, either," said God.

"I wanted something more beautiful," said Mr. Whittle apologetically: "something like heaven."

"Beauty is in the eye of the beholder," said God; "and so am I. And so is heaven," He added.

He was silent for a moment, and Mr. Whittle thought that he could hear Him breathing. But it was Mr. Whittle's own breath that he heard, raucous and difficult. "Well," said Mr. Whittle drowsily, "it's too late now."

"Do you think it polite," asked God, "to slam the door in my face?"

"I didn't slam the door," said Mr. Whittle. "I'm sorry."

And he added simply:

"I have had a hard day."

"I know," said God.

"You must not think I am unkind," He said; "I am only indifferent. That does not mean that I am without love; but My love, unlike yours, must stretch to infinity, and last forever. Otherwise, where am I?"

A star flashed downward in the sky, leaving a trail of silver behind. Is that me? Mr. Whittle wondered.

"Did you wish on it?" God asked gently.

"I forgot," said Mr. Whittle. "It went so fast."

"It's not too late," said God.

"Then," said Mr. Whittle with all his heart, "I wish I could see Amanda again, before I die."

The silver radiance grew brighter and brighter; it seemed to take up all of space and time. Mr. Whittle shut his eyes, to keep out the light which hurt him; then he peered cautiously out again, through half-open lids. He seemed to be in his own room, in his house, in Rivertown; and someone was leaning over his bed, smiling at him. It was Amanda; and behind her was someone else . . . the doctor; he remembered now. He felt cool and weak, and able to breathe again. . . .

"The crisis is over," said the doctor with satisfaction.

Mr. Whittle's hand reached out in a feeble way toward his wife. "He said it wasn't too late," he whispered.

She took his hand in both of hers, and kissed it. Then, laying her head on the cover beside him, for the first time, she wept bitterly.

"Can't you wear your rubbers, at least," she sobbed, "when you go out in the rain?"

A NOTE ON THE TYPE

This book was set on the Linotype in *Scotch*, a type-face that has been in continuous service for more than one hundred years. It is usually considered that the style followed in our present-day cuttings of Scotch was developed in the foundry of Alexander Wilson and Sons of Glasgow early in the nineteenth century. The new Wilson patterns were made to meet the requirements of the new fashion in printing that had been set going at the beginning of the century by the "modern" types of Didot in France, of Bodoni in Italy, and of Baskerville in England. It is to be observed that the *modern* in these matters is a modernity of A.D. 1800, not of today.

The book was manufactured by The Plimpton Press, Norwood, Massachusetts, and was designed by W. A. Dwiggins.